Short Readings for Sunday

SALZWASSER
VERLAG

Gale R. Rhoades

Short Readings for Sunday

Reprint of the original, first published in 1864.

1st Edition 2022 | ISBN: 978-3-75259-484-3

Verlag (Publisher): Salzwasser Verlag GmbH, Zeilweg 44, 60439 Frankfurt, Deutschland
Vertretungsberechtigt (Authorized to represent): E. Roepke, Zeilweg 44, 60439 Frankfurt, Deutschland
Druck (Print): Books on Demand GmbH, In de Tarpen 42, 22848 Norderstedt, Deutschland

Short Readings

FOR

Sunday.

Short Readings

FOR

Sunday.

BY THE AUTHOR OF

"Footprints in the Wilderness."

Oxford and London

1864.

CONTENTS.

LIST OF ILLUSTRATIONS.

I.

Light and Darkness.

HAVE you ever seen the sun rise? If not, I would advise you to get up some fine morning before daybreak on purpose to see it. If you live in the country, and can get on a hill or any high ground, you will see it far better than you could do anywhere else; and if you turn towards the east, you will find the darkness grow less and less in that direction, until a faint streak of light appears just where the earth and sky seem to meet. You must watch this streak; and as it grows gradually wider and brighter the daylight will grow stronger and stronger, until the sun itself comes up by degrees, rising higher every minute, until heaven and earth are filled with its glory. It "cometh forth as a bridegroom out of his chamber, and rejoiceth as a giant to run his course. It goeth forth from the uttermost part of the heaven, and runneth about unto the end of it again: and there is nothing hid from the heat thereof[a]."

Just look around when the sun has fairly risen, and it will scarcely seem like the same world that lay in gloom and darkness so short a time since. The surrounding objects, which you then saw so dimly through the twilight that they looked almost like shadows, will now stand out clear and distinct in the broad light of day, and it will seem as if everything had just woke up from sleep, and was rejoicing in the brightness and warmth. You know what a difference the sunshine makes to us all; how much more cheerful and happy we feel when it is bright and sunny, than we do when it is dull and the clouds are dark and heavy. And more than this, you know that it is the sun which brings out the leaves and blossoms, and ripens the fruits

[a] Ps. xix. 5, 6.

of the earth. I could tell you, too, of many wonderful things which are done by means of the light and heat derived from it; but I will only remind you that without it few things could live, and none would ever come to perfection.

For although we should all of us think upon the wonderful works of God, and learn all we can about them, that we may see His power and goodness in them, I want you to see in them something more than just what you look upon with your bodily eyes—something that will teach you about heavenly things. And so, when you look up to the glorious sun, which gives light and life to this world, and which we can all feel and see shining upon us outwardly, I would have you think of the Sun of Righteousness which shines into our souls—I mean the Lord Jesus Christ.

When He was living in this world, and teaching His disciples, He very often made use of earthly things to help them to understand and remember what He said about spiritual things; and if you read carefully all He says about light and darkness, you will see that by 'light' He means 'holiness,' and by 'darkness' He means 'sin.' He says, in the Gospel of St. John, "If any man walk in the day, he stumbleth not, because he seeth the light of this world. But if a man walk in the night, he stumbleth, because there is no light in him[b]." Now you know that if any one walks about in broad daylight he can see his way before him, and avoid any danger he may encounter in it, or at any rate prepare to meet it. But it is not so with one who walks in the dark. He cannot tell whither he is going, and may wander far out of the right road, or lose his way entirely. He is full of fear and uncertainty, and may run into all sorts of danger without knowing that he is doing so or being able to escape from it: he may even miss help, if it be close at hand, because he cannot see it, and so be lost altogether.

[b] John xi. 9, 10.

Well, this is just what happens to people who walk in spiritual darkness—that is, those who live in sin. They wander further and further from the path of holiness, till they hardly know right from wrong, and fall into all kinds of sin and evil, far worse than any bodily danger; and Satan, who leads them astray, tries to prevent their seeing that God is ready and willing to help them if they turn to Him. So they go on from bad to worse, "walking in darkness," until death leaves them no time for repentance.

Of such as these our Lord says they "loved darkness rather than light, because their deeds were evil[c]." But they who walk in His ways need have no fear; for He Himself says, "I am the Light of the world: he that followeth Me shall not walk in darkness, but shall have the light of life[d]." Just as the sun is the light of this world, and enables us to walk about in safety, and see whither we are going and what we are doing, so the Lord Jesus is

[c] John iii. 19. [d] John viii. 12.

the "true Light, which lighteth every man that cometh into the world[e]," and shines into the souls of all those who are willing to be led by Him. He shews them the snares and temptations that the Evil One places in their path, and enables them to avoid them or delivers them out of them. He helps all who look to Him not only to find the narrow way which leadeth unto life, but also to walk in it.

St. Paul bids us "walk as children of light[f];" that is, to live as the children of God should live. Will you not try to do so? If you do not love sin, you need not walk in darkness. If you feel your sinfulness, ask God to cleanse you from your sins by the precious Blood of His dear Son. Ask Him to give you grace to put away from you the works of darkness, and to grant you the light of His Holy Spirit, that by His help you may so steadily walk in His ways in this world, that by His mercy you may finally

[e] John i. 9. [f] Eph. v. 8.

reach that blessed home where there is no darkness,—that fair city which hath "no need of the sun, neither of the moon, to shine in it: for the glory of God doth lighten it, and the Lamb is the light thereof[g]."

"The light of truth to us display,
Make us to know and choose Thy way;
Plant holy fear in every heart,
That we from God may ne'er depart."

[g] Rev. xxi. 23.

II.

The New Year.

THE New Year! What a season of general rejoicing it is! How many voices usher it in with the words,—old indeed, but full of kindly feeling,—"A happy new year to you!" How many families, divided and scattered through the length and breadth of the land, who seldom—perhaps never—meet together at any other time, gather round the firesides of rich and poor on that day, with hearts full of joy and thankfulness!

Now let us see how the Church keeps New Year's Day. If we turn to the Prayer-book, we shall find it dedicated to the service of God—set apart and appointed to be observed, or kept holy, as the Feast of the Circumcision. And well and wisely has this day been selected for its observance, for two reasons.

First, because circumcision was the rite by which children and converts were admitted into the Jewish Church, as Christians are by Baptism made members of the holy Catholic Church: and it thereby teaches us a lesson of obedience, by shewing us how our blessed Saviour, who was the only-begotten Son of God, and equal with Him, became obedient to the ordinances given to man by His Father, although there could be no need for His doing so, except as an example to us. Secondly, because it brings our baptismal vows and obligations more clearly before us, by identifying the commencement of the new year with that holy Sacrament; reminding us, that as every succeeding year is the beginning of a fresh term of our natural life, so Baptism is the beginning of our spiritual life.

We are taught that two things are required on the part of those who come to this Sacrament—repentance and faith; and a little thought will shew us how this also applies to the subject. We can none of us look back upon the past month—much less a whole year—without finding cause for much sorrow and shame. Sins of omission and commission; sins of heart, lip, and life; uncharitable thoughts, angry words, and unkind actions; forgetfulness of God, and neglect of the means of grace which He has given us,—all these, and many more, rise up in judgment against us. Well is it, therefore, that we should be brought into the immediate presence of God at that season, to "acknowledge and bewail our manifold sins and wickedness, which we, from time to time, most grievously have committed, by thought, word, and deed, against His Divine Majesty" during the year that is past; and to ask His direction and assistance through the one which lies before us, trusting in the promise of His mercy and forgiveness to those who "truly and earnestly repent them of their former sins, and stedfastly purpose to lead a new life."

We must remember, too, that repentance

means something more than the mere being sorry for our sins: it means the actual forsaking them, without which there can be no real repentance.

> "'Tis not enough to say,
> We're sorry, and repent;
> Yet still go on, from day to day,
> Just as we always went.
>
> "Repentance is to leave
> The sins we loved before,
> And shew that we in earnest grieve
> By doing so no more."

And we can only hope to do this by the grace of God, which we must seek to obtain by constant and earnest prayer, and which He will surely give us if we ask it in humble faith.

We have need of faith, too, in the concerns of daily life. We none of us know what may befal us in the course of the new year; but we do know that whatever happens to us is of God's ordering, and that whatever He is pleased to send, is the very best thing for us: so we must just leave all to Him—cast our care upon Him, because He careth for us and knows what is good for us.

We all have daily and hourly blessings to be grateful for; and we have, many of us, received special gifts for which we can never be grateful enough. Just try, each one of you, to count up the mercies He has bestowed upon you during the past year, and then think how many—or rather, how few—they would have been if He had only given you what you deserve. Think of all He has done for you, and how little you have done for Him; how often you have disobeyed Him, how little you love or try to please Him; and pray that He will fill your hearts with love and gratitude to Him, and enable you to shew forth your thankfulness not only in word, but in deed—in every action of your lives.

Pray that each succeeding year which He may permit you to see, may find you further advanced in the "narrow way which leadeth unto life," and nearer to that heavenly kingdom into which we all hope to be admitted, through the merits of our blessed Redeemer.

"Help us, O Lord, to watch our hearts,
And to our ways take heed;
That we with each new year that comes
A holier life may lead.

"Help us to leave our sinful ways;
Make us to love Thee more;
And every year to try and serve
Thee better than before."

III.

The Guiding Star.

"THE heavens declare the glory of God: and the firmament sheweth His handywork[a]." Do not these words come into your mind as often as you look up on a clear night, and see the sky above you spangled with thousands of stars, glittering like diamonds, and think that God made them?—that, countless as they seem, "He telleth the number" of them, and "calleth them all by their names[b]?" Is it not wonderful to think that those very stars have been shining on, just where He placed them, night after night, and year after year, ever since the world began; and will shine on, unchanged, in their appointed courses, fulfilling His will, until that day wherein "the stars shall fall

[a] Ps. xix. 1. [b] Ps. cxlvii. 4.

THE GUIDING STAR.

The Wise Men of the East.

from heaven, and the powers of heaven shall be shaken[c]," and the "Son of Man shall come in the glory of His Father with His angels[d]," to judge both the quick and the dead?

When I was a little child, nothing pleased me so much as to stand at the window when it began to grow dark, and watch for the stars: I well recollect how delighted I was to see them come forth, one by one, till the whole heaven was lighted up with them. I daresay you love to do so too. Now should you not think it very strange if, some night when you were looking at them, one star were to leave its place among the rest, and move on and on as if it were travelling to some distant country?

Well, this strange thing did happen, nearly two thousand years ago, in a land very far away from this, where some wise men were watching the stars;—not, as you do, for pleasure, but because they had heard that about

[c] Matt. xxiv. 29. [d] Matt. xvi. 27.

that time a wonderful star would appear, which was to proclaim, or shew forth, the birth of some remarkable person—a king or ruler of the Jews. You may imagine that they watched for it eagerly, for when they saw it "they rejoiced with exceeding great joy;" and when the star began to move they followed it, believing that it would lead them to the place where this king was: and so it did.

It went before them through all their journey, and at last stood still over a lowly cattle-shed, within which they found Him whom they had come so far to seek, even Jesus Christ, the King of Glory, the Saviour of the world; and having found Him, they fell down and worshipped Him, presented their costly offerings to Him, and then departed, full of joy and thankfulness, to their own land.

You all know this history well, I am sure; but have you ever thought about it so as to learn anything from it? If not, try to do so now.

First of all, there is the journey. You

know that we are not to live in this world for ever; that we are only passing through it on our way to heaven; so that our life is like a journey, and we, like these wise men, need something to guide us safely on our way. They were led by a bright star, and so are we. Not such a star as that which shone in the heavens above them at Bethlehem, but one which is a far surer guide, even the Lord Jesus Himself, who is "the bright Morning Star[e];" the "true Light which lighteth every man who cometh into the world[f];" and who hath given us the promise, "He that followeth Me shall not walk in darkness, but shall have the light of life[g]."

Then we see that the wise men must have followed the star very closely: not shrinking from the dangers and difficulties of the way, not tempted by anything to lose sight of it; but moving steadily on, keeping their eyes fixed upon it, and carefully following where-ever it led them: for if they had not done so,

[e] Rev. xxii. 16. [f] John i. 9. [g] John viii. 12.

they would never have found their way to Bethlehem. And that is how we must follow our blessed Lord, if we would have Him lead us to His home in heaven.

Not suffering the cares of this world and the deceitfulness of riches to draw our hearts away from Him; not giving up trying to follow Him because we find it hard and difficult to do so; but keeping our eyes fixed on Him, we must strive to follow daily more closely in the blessed steps of His most holy life.

Even a little child may do this, by trying to keep His commandments and follow His example,—by trying to become gentle, humble, obedient, and holy, as He was. I need not tell you that trying alone will not make you so; for we "have no power of ourselves to help ourselves;" but if you ask Jesus to help you, and He sees that you are really and earnestly struggling against your sins and faults, and trying to love Him more and serve Him better, He will not only shew you the way in which you should walk, but give you grace and strength to walk in it, and finally receive you into that place which He has prepared in His Father's house, His home in heaven, for those who have truly and stedfastly followed Him here on earth.

"As with gladness men of old
Did the guiding star behold;
As with joy they hailed its light,
Leading onward, beaming bright;
So, most gracious Lord, may we
Evermore be led by Thee.

"Holy Jesus, every day
Keep us in the narrow way;
And, when earthly things are past,
Bring our ransomed souls at last
Where they need no star to guide,
Where no clouds Thy glory hide."

IV.

The Great Physician.

I DARESAY you all know that the word "physician" is only another name for a doctor. It really means a "healer," that is, one who heals people, or cures them of their wounds and diseases.

There was once a Great Physician who went about doing good and healing all who came to Him. No matter what their complaint was, or how long they had been suffering from it, He always cured them, even after all other doctors had tried in vain to do so; and He was so gentle and compassionate that He never turned away any one, however poor and helpless they might be.

One day there came a poor man and begged Him to heal him. He was afflicted with a fearful disease called leprosy, which was so loathsome and contagious that those

THE GREAT PHYSICIAN.

who had it were shunned by everybody, and were not allowed even to live amongst other people. What a sad, solitary life he must have led! How lonely he must have felt, parted from all belonging to him, and having none of those he loved near him, only those who were sufferers like himself! You may be sure he had tried every means of getting cured, but nothing had done him any good.

Well, he must have heard somehow of the wonderful cures which this Great Physician had performed upon other people, for he told Him that he knew He could heal him if He would, and besought Him to do so; and He pitied the poor man, and restored him to health. Only think what a great blessing that was, and how thankful he must have been for it.

Now this Great Physician still lives, and is still able and willing to heal all who go to Him, for it was no other than the Lord Jesus Christ.

Perhaps you will say that you are quite

well and have no disease of which to be cured; but you are, or may be ill sometimes, and then you must pray to Him to heal you. For although the doctor may give you medicine, and do all he can to cure your sickness, it will be of no use unless it pleases God to bless the means used; it is He who really heals you.

But if you have no bodily disease, there is one far worse, with which we are all afflicted, I mean sin, which destroys our souls; and it is very like the dreadful disease which the poor man had of whom I have been telling you. I have said before that it was called leprosy, and it began with a small spot, which spread, and spread, until it covered the whole body, and could not be got rid of. This is just what sin is to our souls. We begin by committing one little sin, and that one leads to another, and that again to many more, and so we go on getting worse and worse, until sin has made our whole soul as foul and loathsome as leprosy did the body.

There is only one cure for this. We must just do as this poor leper did; we must go to Jesus, the Great Physician, and ask Him to heal us. He alone can cure our bodily sicknesses, and He alone can cleanse our souls from sin. He will do it too, if we go to Him believing that He can and will do so. He is just as powerful and just as compassionate now as He was then; for you know He is "the same yesterday, to-day, and for ever [a];" and He never turns away any who go to Him confessing their sinfulness and repenting of their sins. He has said, "Him that cometh to Me, I will in no wise cast out [b]." Go to Him then, as this poor man did, and ask Him to heal you. Say, as he did, "Lord, if Thou wilt, Thou canst make me clean [c];" and try to believe it in your heart as well as say it with your lips, remembering His own gracious promise, "Whatsoever things ye desire, when ye pray, believe that ye receive them, and ye shall have them [d]."

[a] Heb. xiii. 8. [b] John vi. 37.
[c] Matt. viii. 2. [d] Mark xi. 24.

You may fancy that because you are only children you are not sinful enough to need such cleansing; but this would be a sad mistake. Just think for a moment what God requires of all His children. Think of the pattern He gives us in His dear Son,—how pure and holy, how meek and gentle He is, and how little like Him you are,—and you must surely feel how sinful you are, how different from what He would have you to be. Pray to Him to "cleanse the thoughts of your hearts by the inspiration of His holy Spirit;" to heal all the diseases of sin, and keep you pure for the time to come; that being cleansed from all sin by His precious blood, you may be found worthy to dwell with Him for ever in His heavenly kingdom.

"O Saviour, make us more and more
  Our sinfulness to feel,
And lead our trembling steps to Thee,
  For Thou alone canst heal.

"Help us to come to Thee in faith,
  And cleanse us from all sin;
O, by Thy Holy Spirit make
  And keep us pure within."

WEEDS.

V.

Weeds.

EVERYONE knows what weeds are: and though they are not useful like herbs, or beautiful like flowers, how, if they be left to do so, they will overgrow both; till, if they do not actually kill them, they choke and hinder their growth, and so prevent their being either useful or beautiful.

You have, I daresay, all of you, had a garden of your own to take care of some time in your lives. Or if not, you may have been set to pull up weeds in somebody else's, and therefore know how quickly they grow, and what tiresome work weeding often is. For unless the weeds are rooted up as soon as they make their appearance, while they are young and small, they strike deeper and deeper into the earth, which gets dry and earth in summer, He will send down His Holy Spirit to soften and refresh them, as the dew and rain moisten the parched ground.

And if we do not seem to get on very fast, we must not be discouraged, but go on patiently and perseveringly, trying, and trusting in Him. But if by His grace we are enabled to overcome any of them, we must not think of it as our own doing, and feel satisfied with ourselves, for Christ tells us, "Without Me ye can do nothing[c];" and, "When ye shall have done all those things which are commanded you, say, We are unprofitable servants: we have done that which was our duty to do[d]:" but give God the glory, for it is He who "worketh in you both to will and to do of His good pleasure[e]."

> "We of ourselves can nothing do,
> But all on Thee depend:
> Thine is the work and wages too,
> Thine both the way and end."

[c] John xv. 5. [d] Luke xvii. 10. [e] Phil. ii. 13.

THE HOUSE OF GOD.
Jacob anointing the Stone.

VI.

The House of God.

WE read of one who, in olden time, was obliged to leave his father's house, and wander forth to seek another home for himself in a far-off land. The journey before him was long and wearisome, and he knew not what might befal him by the way: but he had acted in obedience to the wishes of his parents, and had set out with his father's parting blessing upon his head, so he went cheerfully on in his appointed path. He journeyed on until the sunlight faded and the shades of evening gathered round him, and then he halted: and as the night closed in, the lonely wayfaring man lay down to sleep in the wilderness, with a stone for his pillow, and the blue sky above with its shining stars looking down upon him as he lay there slumbering peacefully, with his staff and scrip beside him, ready to pursue his pilgrimage on the morrow.

As he slept he dreamed, not of the home and the parents he had left so lately, but of a wonderful ladder, reaching from earth to heaven, upon which the angels of God were ascending and descending. And his heavenly Father Himself talked with him, and comforted him, and promised him His blessing and protection. Well might he awake full of awe and reverence, to consecrate the place by setting up an altar there, and vowing a vow unto the Lord! Well might he in love and faith go on his way rejoicing!

You may by this time have found out that this wayfarer was the patriarch Jacob; and will, perhaps, wonder what all this can have to do with you: but it seems to me that the lesson to be drawn from it will apply to all of us. We, like Jacob, have set out on a long journey, full of perils and difficulties, even the journey of life; and seek a home in "the land that is very far off," even the house of many mansions, in which, our Saviour tells us, He is gone to prepare a place for us[a]. Like him, also, we know not what may lie before us; but God has provided rest and refreshment, both spiritual and bodily, for us by the way, by giving us His blessed Word, His holy day of rest, the ordinances of His holy Church, and the ministrations of those whom He has chosen and set apart as His appointed ministers, and specially endued with His Holy Spirit.

Now do you think we all use these great blessings rightly? I fear not. Jacob worshipped God devoutly in that solitary place, which he called "the House of God;" but I am sure your own conscience will remind you that when you have attended in His holy house you have not done so, but have drawn near to Him with your lips when your heart was far from Him. Too many of you are staring about, or whispering and laughing, instead of attending to the service; or if you

[a] John xiv. 2.

are not outwardly irreverent, your mind is distracted, and full of wandering thoughts. You must surely forget whose house and whose presence you are in when you behave in this manner, and how displeasing such conduct must be to Him of whom we are told, "They that worship Him must worship Him in spirit and in truth[b]."

Perhaps you will say, "If I could see God, as Jacob did, I should be reverent and devout too." But although you cannot see Him with your bodily eyes, He is nevertheless present with you; for Jesus says, "Where two or three are gathered together in My Name, there am I in the midst of them[c]." Remember, too, His rebuke to the doubting Apostle St. Thomas, "Because thou hast seen Me, thou hast believed: blessed are they that have not seen, and yet have believed[d];" for it applies equally to you.

I do not say that you can always help your thoughts wandering; but you *can* try to pre-

[b] John iv. 24. [c] Matt. xviii. 20. [d] John xx. 29.

vent their doing so, by striving to realize His presence with you; by trying to join heartily in the prayers and praises of the congregation, and listening attentively to the reading of His Holy Word, or the instructions given you by His ministers: and then He will bless the means of grace which He Himself has ordained, and help you to improve them.

> "Oh, may a sense that Thou art nigh,
> Our youthful hearts with awe inspire;
> Check the vain thought, the wand'ring eye,
> And banish every wrong desire."

Above all, pray earnestly for grace to worship Him with inward devotion of spirit, as well as outward prostration of body: and beg Him to give you such a sense of His presence as will enable you to say with Jacob, "Surely the Lord is in this place; and I knew it not. . . . This is none other but the house of God, and this is the gate of heaven[e]."

[e] Gen. xxviii. 16, 17.

"And whilst, with mingled love and fear,
We, in Thy service, bear our part;
Give us, O Lord, the hearing ear,
Give us the understanding heart.

"Give us, through Jesus' dying love,
To feel our countless sins forgiven
So shall Thine earthly temple prove,
In very deed, the gate of heaven."

VII.

Truthfulness.

HOW very rare it is to find a perfectly truthful person. And by "truthful" I do not mean a person who is only not in the habit of lying, but one who would on no account tell a falsehood;—one whom nothing would induce to say anything that is not strictly true. It is very seldom indeed that we meet with any one who is as truthful as that: and yet if we would please God we ought every one of us to be so. God hates a lie; and you know He tells us in His Holy Word that the devil is the father of lies. He says, "There is no truth in him. When he speaketh a lie, he speaketh of his own; for he is a liar, and the father of it[a]." All liars, therefore, are the children of the devil, not God's children, and shall, we are told,

[a] John viii. 44.

"have their part in the lake which burneth with fire and brimstone[b]." Is not this a fearful thing to think of?

But if you really love God, you will care even more about displeasing Him than being punished for doing so. He loves you far better than you can ever love Him, far better even than your earthly parents do, (and they love you better than anybody else); and He would have you pure and holy, even as He is holy. Surely you would not willingly grieve Him? Try, then, to be truthful. Think how hateful a lie must be in His sight who is the Truth itself; and let nothing tempt you to tell one. Remember that every lie you tell will be written down in His book, and brought against you at the day of judgment.

Remember, too, that He hears every word you say, and although you may deceive other people you cannot deceive Him: and let this thought help you to speak the truth at all times—even when you have been doing wrong

[b] Rev. xxi. 8.

and a lie might save you from punishment. Think that God is listening to you, and you will not dare to do otherwise.

> "Oh, how could children tell a lie,
> Or cheat in play, or steal, or fight,
> If they remembered God was by,
> And had them always in His sight."

You may perhaps think, if you are tempted to tell a falsehood, that just *one* will not matter so much: but indeed it will. People who once begin to tell lies cannot stop at 'just one.' Those who tell one lie to conceal a fault are often obliged to tell more to avoid being found out in the first. They are ashamed or afraid to own that they have told an untruth, and so go on from one to another until they become regular liars. And Satan will put all sorts of temptations and opportunities in their way, until they get into such a habit of lying that they really hardly know when they are doing so,—whether they speak the truth or not.

I should hope you would never, any of

you, come to such a sad state as this; but even if you do not you may be very untruthful, although you may never actually tell a lie—for lies may be *acted* as well as spoken. If, for instance, another person were to be charged with a fault or sin which you have committed, and you were to suffer that person to be suspected of it or punished for it, instead of confessing that you did it, that is just as bad as lying—just as much a lie in God's sight as if you denied having done it in words. If, by words or manner, you try to make people believe anything contrary to the simple truth, it is just the same thing in reality as telling an untruth with your lips, and quite as displeasing to the Lord who "searcheth all hearts, and understandeth all the imaginations of the thoughts[c]."

If you have done wrong, do not try to conceal it, but tell the truth about it honestly and boldly. Surely the feeling that God was angry with you for telling a lie would be far

[c] 1 Chron. xxviii. 9.

worse to bear than any punishment that could be inflicted upon you; surely you should be more afraid of displeasing Him than of any one else's anger. Try to be truthful, then; for "lying lips are abomination to the Lord[d]." Try to follow the example of the blessed Jesus, "who did no sin, neither was guile (or deceit) found in His mouth[e]." Ask Him to make you pure and holy, like unto Him; to cleanse and sanctify your heart,—for we know that "the imagination of man's heart is evil from his youth[f],"—that by His grace you may not sin against Him with your lips, but speaking the truth in all things may glorify Him in your lives, and finally enter that glorious city from which "whosoever loveth and maketh a lie[g]" shall be shut out for ever.

"The wicked father of all lies
 Goes to and fro, and watches nigh;
And He rejoices when he gets
 A Christian child to lie.

[d] Prov. xii. 22. [e] 1 Peter ii. 22.
[f] Gen. viii. 21. [g] Rev. xxii. 15.

"You cannot see the holy God,
Nor that bad spirit tempting you;
But you can watch, and never speak
A word that is not true.

"For Christ, who looks into our hearts,
Sees all we think, hears all we say,
Will surely help us to be good,
If we but watch and pray."

THE BLIND BEGGAR.

VIII.

The Blind Beggar.

I DARESAY you have many a time seen a poor blind man walking about, feeling his way very carefully with a stick, lest he should run against any one, or fall over anything lying in the way, which he could not otherwise avoid, as he cannot see. He is frequently led by a dog, which guides him as well as a child could do; and his dog very often carries in his mouth a little tin cup, to hold any money the passers-by may give his master; and very few pass without dropping something into it.

Well, just such a poor man as this sat one day, many hundred years ago, by the wayside near to the city of Jericho, begging.

Perhaps, if he had lived in these days, he might have been able to do something towards getting his own living; for now, you know, there are many asylums and schools for the blind, where they are taught, not only to read,—which they do by means of books with raised letters cut in wood, which they can feel with their fingers,—but also to knit and net, to make mats, weave baskets, and many other useful things by which they can earn a little money. But in those days it was very different; there were no such places then, and so he could do nothing but beg.

What a weary life his must have been! Never to be able to look upon the faces of those he loved; never to gaze upon the green trees and lovely flowers, the blue sky and the glorious sunshine by day, and the bright stars and the silver moonlight by night, and all that God has given to make this world of ours so beautiful, but to be always in darkness. No difference for him between night and day—nothing but dreary darkness! And then to be obliged to beg his bread from day to day, having nothing to depend upon but what people chanced to give him. Perhaps some days he might get nothing at all, and then he must suffer hunger, and thirst, and weariness, if no one gave him food or shelter. When we think of all this, should it not make us very thankful to God for having given us the blessing of sight?

This poor man, then, was sitting by the wayside begging, mourning probably over his loneliness and helplessness, little thinking that deliverance was so near at hand. There were many persons passing to and fro, for it was the highway to Jerusalem; but suddenly he heard the sound of many feet in the distance, and presently "a multitude passed by." Now he knew that there must be something unusual going on to draw such a number of people together,—just as we do when we see a crowd anywhere,—so he asked what it meant; and they told him that Jesus of Nazareth was passing by.

As soon as he heard that, he called out, "Jesus, Thou Son of David, have mercy on me;" and although those who went before rebuked him, and told him to hold his peace, he paid no attention to them, but went on calling upon Jesus. And it was well that he did, for then our Blessed Lord stood still, and commanded him to be brought; and when he drew near, gladly enough you may be sure, He asked him what he wanted Him to do for him. And he said, "Lord, that I might receive my sight." You know that our Lord granted his prayer; and you may imagine his joy and gratitude at receiving that precious gift of sight. Well might he follow the giver of it, glorifying God. We are not told *how* he knew that Jesus could heal him, but we may be sure that he *did* know it, and believe it too, for our Lord Himself said to him, "Thy faith hath saved thee[a]."

We read in Holy Scripture that all these things are "written for our learning[b]," so there must be some lesson for us contained

[a] Luke xviii. 42. [b] Rom. xv. 4.

in this miracle: let us try to find out what it is.

First, it shews us how ready Jesus is to hear all who call upon Him; and that none, however poor and helpless they may be, ever call upon Him in vain. Surrounded as He was by so great a multitude, you might have thought that amid the noise and bustle of the crowd the cry of the poor blind man would scarcely reach His ear; but it did. And though He must have been weary with a long day's journey, and the people were impatient at this hindrance, He nevertheless stopped and healed him.

So you see what *we* must do when we need help; we must go to Jesus. He is just as near to us now as He was to the blind beggar then; just as able and willing to hear us; and although to try our faith He may not seem to hear us at first, yet if he finds that we go on calling on Him in humble trust, as this poor blind man did, He will hear our prayer at last, and help us as He did him.

And now there is something to be learnt about blindness. You know we may have the full use of our bodily eyes, and yet be very blind for all that. There is a worse kind of blindness than that which deprives us of sight—I mean *blindness of heart;* and this was what our Lord meant when He called the Scribes and Pharisees blind. They could see all His miracles with their outward eyes, but they did not believe in Him in their hearts; and just so we may read God's Holy Word with our eyes, so as to know all about Him, and what He would have us to do, and yet neither believe in Him and love Him, nor do His will. So we must do as the poor blind beggar did. We must go to Jesus, and ask Him to open the eyes of our understanding, that we may see and believe on Him, whom truly to know is everlasting life.

"Open our eyes, O Lord, that we
May see Thee as Thou art;
May read Thy Word to know Thy will,
And do it from the heart."

IX.

Obedience.

IF you were asked what "obedience" means, you would all answer, as readily as possible, "Doing whatever you are told to do, and not doing anything you are forbidden to do;" for it is easy enough to talk about it, but a very different and far more difficult thing to practise it. You would answer rightly too, for obedience does mean minding what is said to you; but it also means something more than this, even the giving up your own will to the will of others.

We are all of us, old and young, selfish by nature, and it is far easier and more pleasant to do what we like, than what we know to be right, or what other people tell or wish us to do. And why is it so, do you think? Because we are all more willing to indulge our own inclinations, and follow the promptings of our own sinful hearts, than to consider what is pleasing to God and obey His commands; more careful to please ourselves than to do His will.

You know we owe obedience first of all to Him, before any human being; and next to Him to our parents, who stand in His place to us on earth; and after them, we are to "submit ourselves to our governors, teachers, spiritual pastors, and masters," as we learn in our "Duty to our Neighbour." This is not an easy thing to do at all times, for it mostly happens that what they forbid is the very thing we have set our mind upon doing, and that what they bid us do is the last thing we wish to do. Do you not often find it so? And when this has been the case, have you not, over and over again, gone your own way and done as you liked, or refused to do what you did not like?

Well, this is just what you must *not* do. God makes the obeying His commands a proof of love to Him:—"He that hath My commandments, and keepeth them, he it is that loveth Me[a]:" and I need scarcely remind you what His commands are on this subject. "Honour thy father and thy mother;" "Children, obey your parents in the Lord: for this is right[b];" "Children, obey your parents in all things: for this is well-pleasing unto the Lord[c]." Not in one or two things which may not be contrary to your own wishes, but in *all* things, whether you like it or not. Hard as this may be, there is one thing which will make it easy to you, and that is—love.

When we love any one very dearly, we do not care what we do for them or how much we give up to please them; we are glad to do anything to shew them how much we love them. And so, if you really love God, you will always be ready to do His will instead of your own: and the more you love your father and mother, the more willingly and cheerfully you will honour them; not

[a] John xiv. 21. [b] Eph. vi. 1, 2. [c] Col. iii. 20

only by obeying their spoken words, but by following out what you know to be their wishes in all things. Remember that the Lord Jesus, the Son of God, to whom all things in heaven and earth are subject, sought not His own but His heavenly Father's will; and not only so, but "was subject" to His earthly parents—a pattern of loving obedience to them; "leaving us an example, that we should follow His steps[d]." Will you not try to do so?

So with God's ministers, and teachers of all kinds. He has put them in authority over you, and in disobeying them, you disobey Him.

Most of you, too, will go one day into service of some sort; and to those God says in His Holy Word, "Servants, obey in all things your masters according to the flesh; not with eye-service, as men-pleasers; but in singleness of heart, fearing God[e]." And again: "Servants, be subject to your masters with all

[d] 1 Pet. iii. 21. [e] Col. iii. 22.

fear; not only to the good and gentle, but also to the froward. For what glory is it, if, when ye be buffeted for your faults, ye shall take it patiently? but if, when ye do well, and suffer for it, ye take it patiently, this is acceptable with God[f]." If, then, those whom you serve are unkind or unjust to you, think of these words, and try to fulfil your duty towards them all the same, that you may please God, if you cannot please them.

You will not always be able to do this, and you cannot hope to do anything without God's help: but you can try, and if He sees that you really do try to obey and please Him, He will enable you to do so more and more. Whenever you feel inclined to be disobedient, whether towards Him, your parents, or your teachers and masters, think of the Lord Jesus, who "pleased not Himself[g]," and try to follow His example, that

[f] 1 Pet. ii. 18—20. [g] Rom. xv. 3.

you may by your actions prove yourselves to be His true disciples.

Do not trust in your own strength and good resolutions, but ask Him to give you the spirit of loving obedience; to pour into your hearts such love towards Him, that you may daily become more and more like Him, and, by the help of His Holy Spirit, in all things obey His blessed will. He will do so if you ask trusting in His gracious promise, "If ye shall ask any thing in My Name, I will do it[h]."

"O holy Lord, content to dwell
In a poor home, a lowly child,
With meek obedience noting well
Each bidding of Thy mother mild;

Lead every child that bears Thy Name
To walk in Thy pure upright way;
To shun the paths of sin and shame,
And humbly, like Thyself, obey."

[h] John xiv. 14.

THE WIDOW'S MITE.

X.

The Poor Widow.

THERE was once a widow who was very poor. She had no husband to work for her, so she was obliged to live, as best she could, on the little she had or could earn for herself; and that was little enough. But although she was so poor, she was one who loved God, and thought more of doing His will and pleasing Him, than of providing for her own comfort or pleasing herself. And how do you think she shewed her love to God? You shall hear.

The city in which she dwelt was a very ancient city; and by far the most glorious, beautiful building in it was, as it ever should be, the House of God. It was always open, so that rich and poor alike could enter in and pray there; and just within the entrance stood a chest, with a hole bored in the lid, to receive the offerings of the people—just as we see an alms-box put up inside most of our churches now,—and this chest was called the "Treasury." It had been placed there many hundred years before, when this holy House needed repairing, to receive the money people offered for that purpose; and still remained, that those who entered the House of the Lord might put into it whatever they wished to devote to His service.

It happened one day, that many rich people passed by and cast their gifts into the treasury—liberal offerings, for they could afford to give largely; and at last came this poor widow, and cast in her gift. I daresay you think that if she was so poor, she could have hardly anything to give: and you are right. Her offering was a very small one—so small, that many people would not have thought it worth giving at all; and perhaps some who saw her casting it into the treasury did think so. But there was One looking on whom she knew not, and in His eyes it was of greater value than any or all of the costly gifts which had gone before it. The Lord Jesus Himself was sitting close by, and when He saw what she had done, He said to His disciples, "Verily I say unto you, that this poor widow hath cast more in, than all they which have cast into the treasury[a]."

Do you wonder how this could be, when she had actually cast in so much less than they had?

Listen to what our Lord says further about it: "For all they did cast in of their abundance; but she of her want did cast in all that she had, even all her living[b]." Now you see why her offering was the most acceptable in the sight of God,—because it cost her some self-denial. The rich people had plenty to spare, and would, perhaps, never miss what they gave; but this poor woman must have denied herself the little food, or comfort of any kind, which this

[a] Mark xii. 43. [b] Mark xii. 44.

money would have procured her, that she might give it to God; so it cost her a great deal.

This teaches us, then, that God does not think so much of *what* we give, as *how* we give it; that is, the feeling, or motive, with which we give it. He expects us all to give something, and would have us give according to our means; whether it be money, time, talent, influence, or anything else with which He has blessed us. From those to whom He has given much, He will expect much: and from those to whom He has given little, something,—as much as they can give. And He will accept the offering of the very poorest, let it be ever so small, if it be given out of love to Him.

Perhaps when there is a collection at church, or any other opportunity of offering anything to God, some of you may let that opportunity pass by, because you have so little to give; because when you see others giving more, you are ashamed to give "only a penny," or "halfpenny," and yet have no more. Whenever you are tempted to do so, just think of this poor widow; and remember that our Lord is nigh, and looking on you now as He was then on her; and will accept the merest trifle you can give, as He did her "mite," if it be given in the same spirit. "If there be first a willing mind, it is accepted according to that a man hath, and not according to that he hath not[c]."

And if you have no money, you must not think that you can give nothing. Think how many people there are in the world who stand in need of help of some kind or other. I am sure there must be some one whom you know, all of you, for whom you can do something: some sick person whom you may help to nurse and wait upon; some old person who cannot see to read for themselves, or perhaps has never learnt to do so, to whom you may read God's Holy Word;

[c] 2 Cor. viii. 12.

some one whom, by denying yourself a little, you may help in some way; and that is as much giving to God as if you gave money.

Pray, then, that He will put His love into your heart to enable you to do this, and help you to give according to the means which He has given you; and in such a spirit that your offering may be acceptable in His sight who "seeth not as man seeth; for man looketh on the outward appearance, but the Lord looketh on the heart[d]."

"The veriest trifle we can give
Will yet accepted be,
If given with a willing heart,
And given, Lord, to Thee."

[d] 1 Sam. xvi. 7.

XI.

Earnestness.

"WHATSOEVER thy hand findeth to do, do it with thy might; for there is no work, nor device, nor knowledge, nor wisdom, in the grave, whither thou goest[a]." So spoke king Solomon, of whom we are told that he was wiser than all men: and surely we need the warning quite as much as they to whom it was given. God has given to every one some work to do; and when people lead an idle life, it is not because there is nothing for them to do, but it is either that they have not found out what their work is, or that they do not choose to do it. You all of you know what work you have to do; but very many of you think that so long as it is done, it does not signify so much *how* it is done. Now this is a great mistake, for whatever is

[a] Eccles. ix. 10.

worth doing at all is worth doing well; and nothing is ever well done that is carelessly done.

There are several ways of doing one's work. Some people will spend double the time they need upon what they have to do, and yet their work will be none the better for it when done, because they have been idling over it, or thinking of something else while they were about it. Others will do as much again in the same time, but although it will be got through much sooner, it will be no better done, because they have finished it too quickly to do it properly, and have done it in a hasty, slovenly manner. But there are others still who set to work cheerfully, and keep their minds fixed on what they are doing while they are about it; not wasting a minute of time, but steadily doing their very best. These last are sure to succeed, because they are in earnest.

And the reason why we should try to be in earnest is, that God gives us work to do, that we may prove our love to Him by the manner in which we do it. If you do anything for any one whom you love very much, it does not seem a trouble to you; or if it really be so, you do not mind it, but rather take pleasure in shewing your affection for the person you love, by the time and labour you bestow on it, and the pains you take to do it as well as you possibly can;—as if your heart worked as well as your hands.

Now I know you will agree with me, that we ought to do more for God than we would for any earthly friends, however dear to us they may be; that we ought to care more about pleasing Him than pleasing ourselves, or anybody else. If we would really please Him, then, if we really wish Him to accept and bless our endeavours to serve Him, we must do the work He has given us heartily and earnestly. It is written of King Hezekiah, "In every work that he began in the service of the house of God, and in the law, and in the commandments, to seek his God, he did it *with all his heart*, and prospered[b]." Just so will it be with us.

When you are at work, think of this: and instead of looking upon it as a task, to be hurried over and got rid of as soon as possible, try, whatever your work may be, and whether you like it or not, to think that you are doing it for God, and do it heartily as unto the Lord. Try to remember that His eye is upon you, and do it as carefully and thoroughly as you would if you saw Him standing by and watching you all the time; and make it a rule never to begin anything without first asking a blessing on it, for without His blessing nothing can prosper.

If you really love God, you will thus find your duty become a delight to you instead of hard, wearisome labour; and if you are not able to do as much as you would wish for Him, do your best, "with good will doing service, as to the Lord, and not to men[c];" knowing that He will not expect

[b] 2 Chron. xxxi. 21.

[c] Eph. vi. 7.

more from you than you are able to perform, but will accept your service, poor and imperfect though it may be, if it be offered with your whole heart, and you ask Him to do so for Jesus Christ's sake.

> "The task Thy wisdom hath assigned
> O let me cheerfully fulfil;
> In all my works Thy presence find,
> And prove Thy good and perfect will.
>
> Thee may I set at my right hand,
> Whose eyes my inmost substance see;
> And labour on at Thy command,
> And offer all my works to Thee."

XII.

The Voice of God.

WE are told in several places in that part of the Bible which is called the Old Testament, that God "talked" with men. Adam, Noah, Abraham, Moses, Elijah, and many others are mentioned, to whom He gave His commandments by word of mouth; —spoke to them Himself, just as an earthly master tells his servants what he wishes them to do.

You have often read these histories, I am sure; but when you have done so, have you ever thought what an awful thing it must be for any one to hear the voice of the great God, who made heaven and earth, speaking to him? Have you ever tried to picture to yourself how you would feel if He were to speak to you?

THE VOICE OF GOD.
Eli and Samuel.

You may fancy that this could never be, because you are only children; but indeed it did happen to a child who lived many hundred years ago, and his name was Samuel. His mother loved him very dearly, but she was very anxious that he should grow up to love and serve God; so although she was loth to part with him, she took him, when he was very young, to His holy House, and after she had solemnly dedicated her child to His service, left him with His minister to be brought up for it: and he ministered before the Lord.

One night, just as he was lying down to sleep, he heard a voice calling him; and thinking it was his teacher's voice, he got up and ran to him to ask what he wanted with him. Eli (for that was his teacher's name) told him he had not called, and bade him lie down again: and he did so. Again he heard the voice, and again he went to Eli; but it was not he who called, so he went back and lay down to sleep once more. A third time the same voice came, and he got up and ran to Eli, as he had done twice before, thinking he *must* have called him. Then Eli knew that it must be God who had called Samuel, and he told him what to answer if the voice came again. It did come, and he said as he had been told to do, "Speak, Lord, for Thy servant heareth[a]." Then God gave him a message for Eli, which Samuel almost feared to deliver; but he obeyed God's voice, and did deliver it in the morning; and grew up in the love and fear of Him who had called him so early, and served Him faithfully all the days of his life.

Are you wondering why I have picked out this story for you? I will tell you why I did so: because, although you may never hear the voice of God with your bodily ears, as Samuel did, He speaks to every one of you all the same, but in a different way: or rather, in more ways than one. He speaks to you by His Holy Word, and by the mouth of His

[a] 1 Sam. iii. 9.

ministers; and in both of these ways His voice comes to those who have "ears to hear" it, whether in His House of Prayer, as it did to Samuel, in their own homes, or in any other place. I wish you would think of this when you are in church, and try to listen to those portions of Holy Scripture which are read, as you would if He Himself were speaking to you; and pay attention to the words of His minister, because He is teaching you through him.

I wish, too, that you would think of it when you read your Bibles at home,—as I hope you all do,—and try to receive its teaching with reverence, as coming from God Himself.

But there is yet another way in which He speaks to us all—I mean by the voice of conscience: and many whose ears are closed to His voice in other ways cannot help hearing it in this. You know this as well as I do; for your conscience must often have warned you before doing anything wrong, that you were going to sin against God: but have you listened to it? You see Samuel not only *heard* His voice but *obeyed* it, although he was almost afraid to do so; probably lest Eli should be angry with him for giving him a message which he knew he would not like to hear. And this is what you must do. When God speaks to you in any way whatever, say, as Samuel did, "Speak, Lord, for Thy servant heareth;" and, like him, also obey.

Do not let the fear of man—what people will say or think of you—prevent you doing what He in His Holy Word, or by His voice in your hearts (your conscience), tells you to do, or urge you into doing what He warns you not to do: but let His will be the one thing you strive to do; His favour the one thing you care most to gain. The more you listen for this voice, the oftener you will hear it, and the more distinctly it will speak: but if you refuse to hear it, it will become fainter and fainter, until at last you will hardly hear it at all.

Think what a dreadful thing it would be

if God were to leave you to go your own way, and fall into sin after sin, because you *would* not listen to His voice of warning or direction! Pray that this may never be your case. Pray that He will give you the hearing ear and the understanding heart, that you may not only listen for His voice, but hear and obey it: that by His grace you may ever hear His call and follow the same, by giving up yourselves obediently to fulfil His holy Commandments.

> "Speak, Lord, and from our earliest days
> Incline our hearts to love Thy ways;
> Oh, let Thy voice now reach our ear!
> Speak, Lord, and let Thy servants hear."

XIII.

Saying and Doing.

YOU may often see two trees of the same sort growing in the same garden or orchard, each of them green, healthy, well-grown, and covered with leaves alike—so much alike that you can see little or no difference between them, and yet find that in reality the one is as valuable as the other is altogether worthless. You will hardly need to be told why this is the case; you will surely guess that it is because the one bears fruit and the other does not. The trees may have been planted at the same time, in the same soil, and have had the same care and attention; the gentle spring showers may have swelled their buds alike; their tender green leaves may have unfolded together in the sunshine, and a fair show of blossom covered each of them alike; and yet when the time of fruit comes the one may be loaded with a goodly crop, while the other, in spite of its early promise, yields none.

Now this is just the difference between saying and doing.

In Holy Scripture, people are often likened or compared to trees and plants. Our Lord Himself uses this comparison in the parable of the "Tares and the Wheat[a]," and the "Barren Fig-tree[b];" He speaks of Himself as the True Vine, and says, "Ye are the branches[c];" He also speaks of a good tree bringing forth good fruit, and a corrupt tree bringing forth evil fruit: but you all understand that He is not speaking of real trees, but of people; and that what He means to teach us is, that just as the value of a tree is known by the fruit it produces, so a person's real character is known by his actions.

You know that, however we may admire the leaves and blossoms of any tree, the fruit

[a] Matt. xiii. 24—30. [b] Luke xiii. 6—9. [c] John xv. 5.

is the most valuable part of it. If you, any of you, had a favourite tree which looked green and flourishing, and bloomed at the proper season, would you not be sadly disappointed if, when the time for it to bear fruit came, you found none upon it? It might go on putting forth its leaves, year after year, as long as it lived, but you would still think it worthless, and perhaps cut it down and chop it up for firewood if it did not bear fruit as it ought to do.

Well, just as we value a tree, not for its leaves and blossoms, but for the fruit it yields, so God values us, not according to what we *say*, but according to what we *do*. We all know that saying and doing are two different things. People may talk a great deal about serving God, and profess to love Him very much, and yet in reality do neither. If they really have the fear and love of God in their hearts they will shew it in their lives; if not, all their professions will be like the leaves and blossoms which never come to anything,

—beautiful enough to look at, but utterly worthless. "By their fruits ye shall know them[d]."

You recollect why our Lord cursed the fig-tree? Because it was barren. He saw it in the distance, and expected to find figs upon it, but when He came to it He "found nothing but leaves only[e]."

Now this is just the case of many persons in this world who seem to be serving God. Their lives appear outwardly fair enough, but in His eyes who "seeth not as man seeth," but "looketh on the heart[f]," and knows our inmost thoughts, they are but barren trees: bearing indeed the leaves of profession, but yielding no real fruit of good works; having a show or "form of godliness," but by their lives "denying the power thereof[g]." Are you like one of these, or are you bringing forth good fruit? Are you contented with saying and seeming, or are you "doers of

[d] Matt. vii. 20. [e] Matt. xxi. 19.
[f] 1 Sam. xvi. 7. [g] 2 Tim. iii. 5.

the word?" "not hearers only, deceiving your own selves[h]?"

You know our Lord says, "Herein is My Father glorified, that ye bear much fruit[i]." Try so to glorify Him. Do not think that it is enough to say your prayers night and morning, to read His Word, and to go to church regularly. The Pharisees did all this, and more; and yet our blessed Saviour told them that their heart was far from God, because they did it to be "seen of men," and trusted in themselves that they were righteous. "Be ye not therefore like unto them[k]," but try to shew forth His praise not only with your lips but in your lives. It is of no use *knowing* His will unless you *do* it. Our Lord says, "If ye know these things, happy are ye if ye do them[l];" and, "Why call ye Me Lord, Lord, and do not the things which I say[m]?" And again, "Not every one that saith unto Me, Lord, Lord, shall enter

[h] James i. 22. [i] John xv. 8. [k] Matt. vi. 8.
[l] John xiii. 17. [m] Luke vi. 46.

into the kingdom of heaven; but he that doeth the will of My Father which is in heaven[n]." So you must strive to be a doer of that will: always remembering that it is only by God's help that you can either become or continue one. Never forget those words of the Lord Jesus, "As the branch cannot bear fruit of itself, except it abide in the vine; no more can ye, except ye abide in Me;" and "He that abideth in Me, and I in him, the same bringeth forth much fruit: for without Me ye can do nothing[o];" but pray to Him for grace to abide in Him. Pray that He will help you to "walk worthy of the Lord unto all pleasing, being fruitful in every good work and increasing in the knowledge of God[p];" that in keeping His commandments you may please Him both in will and deed.

"Help us to praise Thee, gracious Lord,
Not with our lips alone,
But let our love in thought and deed,
As well as words, be shewn.

[n] Matt. vii. 21. [o] John xv. 4, 5. [p] Coloss. i. 10.

"May we not be like barren trees,
Where only leaves are found;
But let Thy Holy Spirit's fruits
In all our lives abound."

ANGER.

Cain and Abel.

XIV.

Anger.

YOU can, most of you, nearly all of you, say the Ten Commandments; but although you say them very often, and hear them read at church at least every Sunday, perhaps you have never thought about them enough to find out what they really mean, and how closely they bear upon the actions and events of our daily lives.

Let us take one of them,—the sixth for instance,—and try to discover how far we are keeping or breaking this commandment which God has given us, "Thou shalt do no murder."

Perhaps you may think that there is no danger of your breaking this commandment, for you are never likely to commit murder. Perhaps Cain once thought so too. Very likely when he was as young as you are he would, like you, have shrunk with horror from the very idea of ever being so cruel and wicked as to take away the life of a fellow-creature; and yet Cain killed his brother. Now let us see how he came to do this. We read in the Book of Genesis that Cain was "a tiller of the ground," and "Abel was a keeper of sheep[a],"—a shepherd; and that they each brought an offering unto the Lord; Cain of the fruit of the ground, and Abel of the firstlings of his flock: each of them the best they had to give.

Now it seems that Abel must have been a better man than his brother, for we find that the Lord accepted his sacrifice, but rejected that of Cain; and St. Paul, in his Epistle to the Hebrews, tells us the reason of this,—"By faith Abel offered unto God a more excellent sacrifice than Cain[b]." Then we read that "Cain was very wroth," which means "angry;" and soon after, that "when they were in the field, he rose up against

[a] Gen. iv. 2. [b] Heb. xi. 4.

Abel his brother, and slew him[c]." Thus we learn that Cain was at first only angry with his brother—jealous, perhaps, of his being better and more pleasing to God than he was; and you see how that feeling of anger got the better of him, and led him to commit the dreadful sin of murder, and draw down God's curse upon himself.

And this will shew you that this commandment means, not only that we must not actually kill any one, but that we must not give way to angry passions and revengeful thoughts, which, if we indulge them, will perhaps drive us on to do so. When people are in a passion they do not know what they are doing; and very often a hasty blow is struck, and they injure or kill another before they are aware of it. And so we must strive against the beginnings of sin, and pray for grace to overcome the first risings of anger, as you know we do in the words of the Litany, "From envy, hatred, malice, and all uncharitableness, good Lord, deliver us."

[c] Gen. iv. 8.

Our blessed Lord Himself teaches us this when He says, "Ye have heard that it was said by them of old time, Thou shalt not kill; and whosoever shall kill shall be in danger of the judgment: but I say unto you, That whosoever is angry with his brother without a cause shall be in danger of the judgment[d]." Remember that God will not accept our prayers, or alms, or services of any kind any more than He did Cain's sacrifice if they are offered with angry passions raging in our hearts; for our Lord tells us, "If thou bring thy gift to the altar, and there rememberest that thy brother hath ought against thee; leave there thy gift before the altar, and go thy way; first be reconciled to thy brother, and then come and offer thy gift[e]."

Try, then, to put away from you "all bitterness, and wrath, and anger, and clamour[f];" and whenever you are tempted to be angry, think of the patience and meekness of Jesus Christ, and pray to Him to help you and

[d] Matt. v. 21, 22. [e] Matt. v. 23, 24. [f] Eph. iv. 31.

make you like Him; to give you "a meek and quiet spirit, which is in the sight of God of great price[g]."

"Give not back the hasty blow,
  Though 'tis given wrongly;
Let the foolish scoffer go,
  Though he tempt thee strongly;
Keep thy gentle Lord in mind,
Who was always meek and kind."

[g] 1 Pet. iii. 4

XV.

The Precious Gift.

THERE was once a poor man who was a cripple, and had been so all his life. From the very day of his birth he had never had the use of his limbs, as you and I have;—could not walk at all, but was always obliged to be carried about. Was it not very sad? And must it not have been a great grief and trouble to him not to be able to walk about like other people? Of course, as he had always been lame he could not do much, if anything, towards getting his living by active employment; so he was carried every day and laid at the gate of the Temple, as the House of God was called at that time, that he might ask alms, or beg, of those who passed in. In those days this holy House always stood open, and people went up to

THE PRECIOUS GIFT.
Peter healing the Lame Man.

pray there two or three times a-day, (for they did not grudge giving up their time to God, as many of us do now-a-days); so I daresay the poor man got many an alms from those who went in and out. Perhaps when they had been praying, and praising their heavenly Father for all His mercies to them, they were more disposed to bestow something on those who needed it, as a proof of their thankfulness.

Well, one day as he was lying there as usual, he saw two men going in at the time for afternoon service, and begged of them, as he did of every one. Now although these men were two of the holy Apostles, they were poor men themselves, and very likely had no money to spare. At any rate they did not give him any; but one of them, fixing his eyes upon him, said, "Look on us:" and he did so, expecting to receive something from them. Then St. Peter, (for it was he,) said, "Silver and gold have I none; but such as I have give I thee: In the name of Jesus

Christ of Nazareth rise up and walk[a]." As he spoke, he took him by the hand and lifted him up; and immediately strength came into his feet, and he not only leaped up and stood but walked, and went into the Temple with them, praising God—as well he might.

I daresay when St. Peter first began to speak to him he felt rather disappointed that he had no money to give him: little thinking that he was about to bestow on him something far better than silver or gold. Can you not imagine what a great surprise and delight it must have been to him, to feel strength and power coming back into the limbs which had so long lain stiff and useless? to know that now he was no longer helpless and a burden to those about him, but able to go where he liked, and help himself? He must indeed have been very grateful to God, who had healed him by their means: and, you see, the very first thing he did was to go into His house and return thanks to Him.

[a] Acts iii. 6.

You have very likely found out by this time that there are two or three things to be learnt from this miracle: but one—and that one I want you to think about now—is, that nobody must think that they have nothing to give, nothing wherewith to help their fellow-creatures, because they may have no money. Our Blessed Lord says to every one of us, poor as well as rich, "Give alms of such things as ye have[b]:" not 'alms of *silver* and *gold*' remember, but "of such things as ye have." Everybody has something. Every child, even, has some gift of God which he can share with those who have it not: each one can do something for somebody; and you know that He is pleased to look upon every service done to another, be it ever such a little one, if done for His sake, as done unto Him.

> "Smallest hands may do Him service;
> Weakest voice His praise may sing;
> More a poor child's simple flowers
> Than the ransom of a king."

[b] Luke xi. 41.

Think of this, then. If you are ever so little, and ever so poor, you will have something to give: find out what it is and give it. This poor man might have remained a cripple all the rest of his life if St. Peter had thought that because he was poor he had nothing to give: but you see he gave what he could; and to the poor lame man his gift was far more precious than silver and gold.

And so it is with us. A kind word, a loving look, a little time or a little trouble bestowed on those to whom we can give nothing else, is often far more precious, and sometimes far more useful to them, than ever so much money would be if we had it to give. There are few, if any, who do not know some one to whom they can give something. If you have health, you can wait on somebody who is ill. If you have time to spare, you can use it for somebody who has not. If you can read, you may read to or teach some one who cannot. There is no little act of kindness, no trifling act of self-denial, even to the giving up your play to do an hour's work, or mind a child, for a neighbour who needs help, that will not be accepted and remembered by God if it be done out of love to Him.

You know who says, "Whosoever shall give you a cup of water to drink in My Name, because ye belong to Christ, verily I say unto you, he shall not lose his reward[c]." Ask Him, then, to give you "such love towards Him," that you may be always ready and glad to help all who need help, for His sake who has said of every service rendered in such a spirit, "Inasmuch as ye have done it unto one of the least of these my brethren, ye have done it unto Me[d]."

"If from your worldly wealth and store
You little have to spare,
Think whether there is nothing more
You can with others share.

"A little help some more may need
Than gold and silver bright;
The loving word, the kindly deed,
Are precious in God's sight."

[c] Mark ix. 41. [d] Matt. xxv. 40.

XVI.

Honesty.

"HONESTY is the best policy" is a very old saying, and a very true one, too. For although dishonest people may prosper for a time, and cheat and even rob others without being suspected of doing so, yet sooner or later they are sure to be found out; and, if they persevere in such ways, come to utter ruin at last. So, even in a worldly sense, it is better to be honest and poor, than to grow rich by robbery and wrong.

But surely Christians should have a better motive than this for being honest. Those who would serve God must keep His commandments; and one of those commandments is "Thou shalt not steal[a]."

It is very sad to think of the hundreds who disobey Him in this respect; notwithstanding

[a] Exod. xx. 15.

HONESTY.
Elisha and Gehazi.

the punishment and the shame and disgrace which always fall upon the thief when the theft is discovered; and, I am sorry to say, some people think more of this than of its being a sin in the sight of God. It is still sadder to know that in London, and many other large cities and towns, children as young as you are regularly brought up to get their living by thieving—taught to thieve just as other children are taught an honest business. How thankful you should be that this is not your lot!

But many people break this commandment who would never think of actually *stealing* anything; for it not only forbids that, but all kinds of cheating, and unfair dealing of every kind. This was the case with Gehazi, the servant of the Prophet Elisha. Naaman, Captain of the host (or army) of the King of Syria, was afflicted with a terrible disease of which none of the physicians of his own country were able to cure him. So, hearing of the wonderful things done by Elisha, he went to him to see whether he could heal him. The Prophet did cure him; and Naaman was very grateful to him, and offered him a large reward, which Elisha steadily refused. This gift Gehazi coveted; so when Naaman had got a little way on his road back, he ran after him, and told him that his master had sent him for a part of it, to give to two of the sons of the prophets who were just come to him. Naaman believed him, and gave him what he asked, supposing that Elisha had really sent him: and he sent two of his servants to help him carry the things back. Gehazi stowed them away very carefully, and when the servants were gone, went in to his master as if nothing had happened; and when Elisha asked him where he had been, he said "Nowhere." He little thought that his master knew what he had been doing so secretly, and that he was telling a lie to hide it from him: he little thought what a fearful punishment was in store for him.

Now you see from this history how any one

may break this commandment without being exactly a thief. Gehazi did not *steal* Naaman's things, but he cheated him out of them by telling a lie. Perhaps some people might think that was not as bad as stealing; but God thought differently, and punished him accordingly. Think of this if ever you are tempted to act dishonestly. Remember that when God says "Thou shalt not steal," He means that you are not only to "keep your hands from picking and stealing," but that you must not deal unfairly by anybody in any way.

If you are sent to buy anything for other people, and spend for yourself any of the money they have given you to pay for it,—if, when you are sent to fetch anything, you take a bit or a sup of it by the way,—if you find anything that does not belong to you, and keep it, instead of returning it to the right owner, when you know whose it is, you are not honest in the sight of God; and if you do these things when you are children, you will go on to something worse when you are older.

When you are grown up you may serve in a shop, or perhaps keep one of your own; and if you then give short measure or light weight,—if you ask people one price for your goods and afterwards make them pay more, or give them wrong change knowingly,—if you do any one of these things, you will be robbing them and sinning against God,—breaking His commandment,—although you may not be guilty of downright stealing.

Again, some of you may go into service: and if you do so, be very careful not to be led into dishonesty in that way. It is a very common thing for servants to think that there is no harm in giving away odds and ends, or scraps of food which do not seem to be wanted; or in entertaining their friends when they come to see them upon whatever may happen to be in the house: but indeed there is harm in it. These things all belong to your master or mistress,—they are not yours;

and it is not right nor honest to use or give away anything belonging to them, unknown to them, and without their permission to do so. They may never miss it or know of it: but the All-seeing God will take note of it, and with Him it will be just as much stealing as if you put your hand in their pocket and robbed them of money.

But it is generally covetousness which leads to this sin in all its forms. People wish for something they do not possess, and steal it: or they want to make more of what they have, and to get rich quickly; and try to do so by any means, fair or unfair. Do not you do so. Remember that God sees all you do, and knows even your most secret thoughts: and let no covetous desires, no prospect of worldly gain, ever tempt you to do anything that you know would displease Him. Do not think, because you see other people doing such things as those against which I have warned you, that there can be no harm in your doing them too. Think, rather, of what such doings are in His sight who is "the Truth," and try to be "true and just in all your dealings," because you belong to Him.

I know that without His help you can do no good thing: but He has promised that help to those who seek it. Pray for it, then. Ask Him to give you such "a fear and love of His holy Name" as will keep you from sinning against Him; that by the help of His grace you may always "serve Him in pureness of living and truth."

"Pilfer not the smallest thing,
Touch it not, howe'er thou need it,
Though the owner have enough,
Though he know it not, nor heed it.

"Upright heart and honest name
To the poorest is a treasure,
Better than ill-gotten wealth,
Better far than pomp or pleasure.

"Poor and needy though thou art,
Gladly take what God has given,
With clean hand and humble heart,
Passing through the world to heaven."

XVII.

The Two Masters.

"NO man can serve two masters: for either he will hate the one, and love the other; or else he will hold to the one, and despise the other[a]."

It is now nearly two thousand years ago that our Blessed Lord spake these words; and yet ever since then people have been, aye, are still trying to do the very thing which He tells us *cannot* be done: and all who do so, find out by experience the truth of the warning, which they must have heard and read many a time, though it may have been unheeded or forgotten by them. I will tell you of one such instance.

There was once a man, who when he was young devoted himself entirely to the service of God, and became one of Christ's ministers.

[a] Matt. vi. 24.

Having done so, he ought to have thought only of serving his Master faithfully, and doing His work: but he was clever and ambitious, and thought more of getting on in the world; so he worked his way up, step by step, until he became a great man, and in time attracted the notice of the King, who made him his friend and counsellor. Courted and flattered by the great, who feared his power or desired favours of him, consulted and trusted by the King, who heaped all kinds of honour and riches upon him, he speedily became one of the wealthiest and most powerful men in the kingdom. But as he rose higher and higher in the favour of his earthly sovereign, he fell away further and further from his Divine Master. Instead of being humble and lowly, and leading a life of simplicity and self-denial, as befitted a follower and minister of Christ, he grew haughty and overbearing, and lived at home and appeared in public surrounded with almost as much pomp and magnificence as the King himself. At last, however, there came a change. The King desired him to do something for him which was directly contrary to the law of God; and when he refused to do it, was very angry with him, and stripped him of all his honours, and as much of his wealth as he could. When he fell into disgrace all his former friends deserted him, and he died at last neglected and miserable; saying with almost his last breath, "Had I but served my God as diligently as I have served my king, He would not have forsaken me in my old age."

You may none of you be tempted as this man was, but you will all have the same two masters as he had to choose between—God and the world; and you must choose either one or the other, for you cannot serve both. Our Lord says, "Ye cannot serve God and mammon[b];" and by "mammon" He means "the pomps and vanity of this wicked world, and all the sinful lusts of the flesh," which

[b] Luke xvi. 13.

you, in your baptism, promised to renounce. All these, pleasant as they may seem, or be, will draw your heart away from God, and hinder, if not entirely prevent, your serving Him. And if you *will* have them at any cost, if you *will choose* them for your portion in this life at all risks, you can have no portion in the life to come: for "the wages of sin is death,"—everlasting death. But if, on the contrary, you choose God for your Master, and try "to serve Him truly all the days of your life" here,—if you will deny yourselves, and take up your Cross, and follow the Lord Jesus, your reward will be far beyond any this world can offer, for "the gift of God is eternal life[e]."

To do this, you will have to struggle against the world, the flesh, and the devil, for all these are your Master's enemies.

"Sinful thoughts of pride and passion,
Greedy wishes, selfish care,
In our human hearts lie hidden,
Ready to awaken there.

[e] Rom. vi. 23.

"Still the wrong way will seem pleasant,
Still the right way will seem hard;
All our life we shall be tempted,
We must ever be on guard."

The "lust (or desires) of the flesh, the lust of the eyes, and the pride of life[d]," will tempt you on every side; but God can and will help you to overcome them, if He sees you are really trying to do so.

But then you must really try, you must give yourselves up to His service. It will not do to serve God on Sunday, and the world all the week, as some people seem to think it quite enough to do. God does not care for half-hearted service like that, and will not accept it. You must serve Him with your whole heart and a willing mind; not as a hard Master, but as a loving Father, a loved and trusted Friend.

The more you love Him, the more anxious and careful you will be to please Him; and the more you try to do this, the more you

[d] 1 John ii. 16.

will feel your own weakness and helplessness, and that without Him you can do nothing. But you know that He has promised His Holy Spirit to those who ask for it: pray often and earnestly for it, trusting in this promise. Ask Him to give you grace "to withstand the temptations of the world, the flesh, and the devil," and so faithfully to serve Him in this life, that you "fail not finally to attain His heavenly promises," through Jesus Christ our Lord.

"Teach us to know and choose the good,
All else to fear and flee;
Help us to trust the Saviour's blood,
And cast our care on Thee."

XVIII.

Meekness.

"BLESSED are the meek[a]." You know who spoke those words; and not only *spoke* them, but *lived* them,—acted them out in His daily life, which was one of such meekness and patience under all sorts of persecutions and injuries as only the Son of God could lead. Our Blessed Lord knew that what people *do* has far more influence over others than what they *say*; and so He left His glorious home in heaven and came and dwelt among men, that He might shew them by His own pure and holy life what theirs must be if they would be the children of their "Father which is in heaven:" that He might leave "us an example, that we should follow His steps[b]."

Now are you all really trying to do this?

[a] Matt. v. 5. [b] 1 Pet. ii. 21.

Are you striving to put away from you all "bitterness, and wrath, and anger, and clamour[e]," and to "walk worthy of the vocation wherewith ye are called, with all lowliness and meekness, with longsuffering, forbearing one another in love[d]." For that is what you must do if you would truly follow and become like Him. And this, not just once now and then, but always, every day and all day long. You may think that it is a very easy thing to do this; but if you try I think you will find that it is not. There are indeed some persons to whom God has given the precious gift of a meek and loving disposition, and those who have it cannot be too thankful for it. But we are, most of us, easily provoked, and find it very difficult to keep our temper amid the crosses and trials that come to every one of us in our daily life.

And why is it so? Because most of us are thinking less of doing God's will than of following our own; and instead of being

[e] Eph. iv. 31. [d] Eph. iv. 1, 2.

contented with having just what He thinks best for us, try to get our own way and do as we like: and when we cannot do this we are vexed and angry,—not, as we ought to be, with ourselves, but with whatever or whoever prevents our doing so. Another reason is that we are all so inclined to be selfish, so apt to think only, or at any rate first, of ourselves, our own comfort, and happiness, and interest, and to lose our temper when anything interferes with either of these things. Perhaps you think that all this is not of so much consequence while you are children, but indeed it is. Do you not know that weeds are easily pulled up when they are small and young, but if they are allowed to go on growing till they become large and strong, it is very difficult, almost impossible sometimes, to get them up at all? And so if you do not try to get the better of your temper, and check your selfishness, while you are young, these faults will grow stronger every day as you grow older, and at last get the better of you. So you must begin at once, and go on striving to attain more and more of the same mind which was in Christ Jesus, even the spirit of love and meekness. And if you do not know how to do this, hear what He Himself says to you, to me, to every one: "Take My yoke upon you, and learn of Me; for I am meek and lowly in heart[e]." So you see He invites all of us, children as well as grown people, to learn of Him: if we go to Him wishing to learn, He will teach us.

It is indeed very difficult to be meek and gentle at all times, but you can at least *try* to be so;—and this is how you must try. When harsh or bitter words are spoken to you, and you feel tempted to give angry words in reply, just think whether, if our Blessed Lord were in your place, He would do so: think of Him "Who, when He was reviled, reviled not again[f]," and ask Him to help you. Remember, too, that "a soft

[e] Matt. xi. 29. [f] 1 Pet. ii. 23.

answer turneth away wrath [g]," and try to give one. You may sometimes be blamed for what is really not your fault, or accused of doing something which you have not done; and what does the Bible tell us about that? It says, "For this is thankworthy, if a man for conscience toward God endure grief, suffering wrongfully. For what glory is it, if, when ye be buffeted for your faults, ye shall take it patiently? but if, when ye do well, and suffer for it, ye take it patiently, this is acceptable with God [h]."

I know that a taunting word or a scornful look is often harder to bear than a real injury. I know, too, that a great many people think that it is only shewing proper spirit to resent these things, and that those who do bear them patiently are weak and cowardly. But which do you think we ought to care for most, what 'other people' say, or what the Lord Jesus says? And He says, "Love your enemies, bless them that curse you, do

[g] Prov. xv. 1. [h] 1 Pet. ii. 19, 20.

good to them that hate you, and pray for them which despitefully use you and persecute you." And why? "That ye may be the children of your Father which is in heaven[1]." Think of His words, and try to put them into practice. Think of His example, and try to follow it; praying constantly and earnestly that He will give you more and more of His Holy Spirit, and make you meek and gentle, and loving like unto Him.

"Make us of one heart and mind,
Courteous, pitiful, and kind;
Lowly, meek in thought and word,
Altogether like our Lord."

[1] Matt. v. 44, 45.

XIX.

"Living with God."

WHERE do you think I first heard those words? and who do you think spoke them? Would you like to know? Listen, and I will tell you.

Some years ago, after I had been very ill, I was taken to the sea-side for change of air; and being too weak to walk about much, I used to go and sit on the beach for hours at a time, sometimes reading, sometimes working, and very often thinking. One morning I had been sitting there a long time, and had read till I was tired; so I shut up my book and amused myself by watching the children who were playing about me. Presently a little girl, who had for some time been playing with her brothers at a little distance, came, followed by her nurse, and sat down beside me.

She was, I should think, between four and five years old, and a nice, bright, intelligent-looking child. We soon became friends, and she prattled away merrily about all sorts of things,—her home, her playfellows, her toys, and her pets, particularly a little dog, which seemed to be a special favourite of hers. At last she mentioned her brothers and sisters, and I asked her how many she had: she said "Six," and directly began to repeat their names: "Willie, and Freddy, and Johnnie, and Harry," pointing to each of her brothers as she named them, "and Jessie and Annie."

"And where are your sisters?" I asked.

She looked up at me for a moment in silence, and then answered, slowly and reverently, "Living with God."

"They are both dead, Ma'am," added the nurse, as if she thought the child's words needed some explanation; "the children all had the scarlet fever just before they came here, and we lost those two. The family are in mourning now," she continued, glancing at the little girl's black frock as she spoke.

I have never seen the little child since then, but I have many a time thought of her words, do often think of them now.

"Living with God." She knew that her sisters were gone from among them, never to return; she knew that she would never see them again here on earth; but she had evidently been taught that they were but gone to their heavenly Father, safe in His keeping; that He was taking care of them just as her own father took care of her: and that was enough for her.

"Living with God." Do not these words make you think of the blessedness of heaven? Of that glorious place, far more beautiful than this world, beautiful as it is; far more lovely than anything you could possibly imagine or dream of, where there is neither sin nor sorrow, hunger nor thirst, pain nor sickness, nothing but peace and joy.

Is it not a great comfort to be able to think of those near and dear ones whom it may have pleased God to take from us by death, as dwelling in that happy home? Would you not like to feel that when you die you will go there too?

Surely you would; but then you must remember, not only what we are told about that happy place, but what we are told about those for whom it is prepared. "Eye hath not seen, nor ear heard, neither have entered into the heart of man, the things which God hath prepared *for them that love Him*[a]." So you see that only those who love and serve Him here will dwell with Him there.

Dear children, are you so living unto God in this world that you may hope to live with Him hereafter in heaven, His dwelling-place? I am afraid not. I fear too many

[a] 1 Cor. ii. 9.

of you live on from day to day, and from year to year, without one thought beyond your daily wants and enjoyments; without one thought of the good and merciful God who supplies all those wants, preserves you in health and safety, and is ever watching over you, soul and body, with the tender care of a Father,—of that loving Saviour whose precious blood was shed to obtain pardon for your sins,—of that Holy Spirit by whose help alone you can perfectly love Him, and serve Him acceptably by walking in the ways of His laws and the works of His commandments.

If this be true of any of you, let it be so no longer. Only think what an awful thing it would be if death were to come upon you suddenly, while you are living without God in the world! Do not fancy because you are young and strong that there is no need to trouble yourselves with such thoughts: that it will be time enough to think about God and heaven when you are going to die.

Remember that "now is the accepted time[b];" that if you would be happy with Him when you die, you must learn to know and love Him while you live. What does He Himself say? "Those that seek Me *early* shall find Me[c];" "Remember thy Creator now, in the days of thy youth[d]." Seek Him now, then, in the diligent use of all the means of grace which He has given you; and learn to live as ever in His sight. The oftener you draw nigh to Him in prayer, the more you study His Holy Word, the more you will know of Him, the better you will love Him; and if by His grace you are enabled thus to live in constant communion with Him in this world, you will not fear to die, for you will know that Christ hath overcome death, and opened to you the gate of everlasting life; you will feel that you are going home to your Father and Friend, and that having striven to do His will, and love and serve Him here on

[b] 2 Cor. vi. 2. [c] Prov. viii. 17. [d] Eccles. xii. 1.

earth, you will, for Jesus' sake, be received to live with Him in Heaven for evermore.

> "O Lord, give all Thy children grace
> The paths of sin to flee;
> Teach them betimes to seek Thy face,
> And live as unto Thee."

XX.

The Good Soldier.

"THE soldiers are coming!" Very often have these words been echoed from mouth to mouth, and whenever you have heard them you have, I am sure, run out to watch them pass by. It is a grand sight to see them marching along to some stirring tune, with their gay uniform, their arms gleaming in the sunshine, and their plumes waving in the wind; and I daresay when you have looked on all this you have thought, "It is a fine thing to be a soldier," without once thinking of all the hardships they have to endure, all the dangers they must encounter. Perhaps, when you have looked on such a scene, it has never reminded you that you too are a soldier,—not exactly like one of these, but a soldier all the same.

The Church of Christ on earth is called the Church Militant, which means 'fighting,' or 'warring against;' and, you know, the Sacrament of Holy Baptism is the one by which we are received into this Church, and all who are thus admitted into it are signed with the sign of the Cross, "in token that they shall not hereafter be ashamed to confess the faith of Christ crucified, and manfully to fight under His banner, against sin, the world, and the devil; and to continue Christ's faithful soldiers and servants unto their life's end."

Now this word "sacrament" means an oath, and more especially refers to the oath of allegiance taken by the soldiers who entered the Roman army and agreed to serve under the Emperor of Rome; just as we, by our baptismal vows, take upon ourselves to serve Christ, to be His "faithful soldiers and servants." Let us see how we are to fulfil these vows.

First of all, the good soldier thinks only of

doing his duty, which is to fight against the enemies of the king whom he serves: and if we would be true soldiers of Christ we must be always striving and fighting against His enemies, "sin, the world, and the devil." We all know that a soldier's life is not one of ease and enjoyment; he is for ever engaged against some foe or other; is often wounded, and sometimes taken prisoner; his comrades fall beside him, and he never knows when *his* turn to die may come. But he does not shrink from all these hardships, he fights on, though he be faint, and wounded, and weary, and his foes fierce and numerous. He knows that his captain's eye is upon him, and he would sooner die than yield, or desert the colours under which he fights.

This is just what we should do. Our spiritual enemies are far more numerous and powerful than any earthly ones. Our sins, our temptations, our evil passions are always trying to get the better of us; but we must resist them with all our might. The more they seem to prevail against us, the harder we must struggle against them and strive to overcome them. Perhaps you do try to do so, and find it such a hard battle that you are almost tempted to give it up. If so, remember that Jesus Himself is the Captain of your salvation; that His eye is upon you, and if you call upon Him He will help you, and give you the victory. "Strive for the truth unto death, and the Lord shall fight for thee[a]." If you are defenceless He can shield you; if you are weak He can strengthen you, and make you conqueror in the end.

Then, again, the good soldier is watchful. He will not leave his post, nor slumber while at it, for he knows that his foes are always near, and ready to take advantage of the least carelessness on his part. He dares not lay aside his arms, or neglect them and leave them to grow rusty, lest the enemy should come upon him unawares and overcome him. So he looks to them often, and is careful to

[a] Ecclus. iv. 28.

keep them clean and bright, that they may be ready for use at a moment's warning. And we must strive to be like him in these respects too, for our foes—pride, vanity, covetousness, envy, selfishness, and many, many others—are always lying in wait, and will rise up against us the moment we forget to watch over ourselves, and will soon vanquish us if they find us unarmed.

> "At our posts beneath His banner
> We must strive, and watch, and pray;
> By the grace of God within us
> Growing better every day."

We are also furnished with weapons, and must keep them clean and bright by constant use, lest they fail us when we need them most. St. Paul tells us what these weapons are: he says, in his Epistle to the Ephesians, "Wherefore take unto you the whole armour of God, that ye may be able to withstand in the evil day, and having done all, to stand. Stand therefore, having your loins girt about with truth, and having on the breastplate of righteousness; and your feet shod with the preparation of the gospel of peace; above all, taking the shield of faith, wherewith ye shall be able to quench all the fiery darts of the wicked. And take the helmet of salvation, and the sword of the Spirit, which is the word of God [b]."

The more frequently a person practises with any weapon the more skilful he becomes in the use of it: and so it is with these spiritual weapons. The oftener we pray, the easier we shall find it to do so: the more we study God's Holy Word, the readier we shall become in the use of it against our adversaries. You know how our Blessed Lord silenced the Tempter with the Word of God, and if you read it carefully and prayerfully, many a time when you are tempted to yield to sin, some text will rise up in your mind and help you to resist it. You must not be discouraged because your foes are many and your strength is small,—no, not even though

[b] Eph. vi. 13—17.

they may sometimes prove too strong for you: you must just go to Jesus and ask Him to give you more strength, and to help you against your enemies; remembering that of yourself you can do nothing, that it is "God which giveth us the victory through our Lord Jesus Christ[c]."

Do not let anything tempt you to grow weary of His service, or to desert it. The battle is long, but it will come to an end some day. The warfare must last all our life; but if we try to continue Christ's faithful soldiers and servants to that life's end, He will give us rest in heaven, where there will be no more sins to fight against, no more temptations to resist, no more pain, or weariness, or hardships of any kind; nothing but peace and joy with Him, the Conqueror, for evermore.

"We are soldiers, doing battle
Day by day, and hour by hour;
Each one with his own temptations
Striving in the Spirit's power.

[c] 1 Cor. xv. 57.

"Still that Spirit stronger groweth
  In the hearts that hold It fast;
He will help us, teach us, crown us,
  More than conqu'rors at the last."

XXI.

The Presence of the Lord.

HAVE you ever heard of a place called Joppa? If you have, you will most likely know that it was the name of a city of Judæa on the coast of the Mediterranean Sea, which is now called Jaffa. If any of you have been at, or lived in a seaport town, you will know that it is very different from any inland place: full of wharves and warehouses; crowded with sailors and seafaring men; nothing but noise and business going on from morning till night, with the lading and unlading of the ships which are constantly coming and going.

Joppa was a trading place of this sort, and at the time of which I am speaking a very flourishing one. Well, all was hurry and bustle there one day; the quays were thronged with people—merchants with their bills of

THE PRESENCE OF THE LORD.

Jonah and the Gourd.

lading—porters hurrying to and fro, or busily employed in removing the bales of merchandise which had just arrived, and delivering those to be sent off,—when a solitary man entered the city from the other side, in hot haste, and hurried on through the streets towards the sea-shore: never stopping until he had reached it. As he hastened along, haggard, breathless, and covered with dust, you might have taken him for some great criminal fleeing for his life, and in fear of being overtaken every moment by the officers of justice in pursuit of him.

On he went, making his way swiftly and silently through the busy crowd, turning neither to the right hand nor the left, intent only upon securing a passage in the ship which was even then on the point of sailing—no matter whither, so that he might but escape from the haunting fear that goaded him on. At last he reached the shore, paid his fare, and leaped on to the vessel, bound for Tarshish, which immediately set sail. But even then he was not at rest: there was no rest, no escape for him, for he was fleeing from the presence of the Lord.

This man was one of God's prophets, named Jonah, who, as you may recollect, was charged by Him with a message to the inhabitants of the city of Nineveh, announcing its destruction, which he was afraid to deliver. The people who dwelt there were so wicked that God was angry with them, and determined to destroy them; and he sent Jonah to tell them so. But it seemed to him so incredible that this great city, which was then the wonder of the world for its extent and magnificence, should be overthrown before forty days more had passed, that he dared not proclaim this terrible judgment lest he should be stoned for a false prophet: and he thought, by leaving the place where he was, to avoid doing it altogether. He forgot that "the eyes of the Lord are in every place, beholding the evil and the good[a];" that God is present everywhere, and

[a] Prov. xv. 3.

wherever he went, His eye would be upon him by day and by night: and you know that the punishment of his disobedience, which he vainly sought to escape, overtook him at last.

I daresay you have heard or read this story nany times; and you may perhaps, when you did so, have wondered how Jonah could be so wicked and foolish: but have you ever thought about the lesson it is meant to teach us? have you ever asked yourself how often you have done the very same thing?

We are all too apt to forget that God is about our bed, and about our path, and spies out all our ways; that He knows the very thoughts of our hearts before we can utter them in words. I am sure if we remembered it a little oftener we should all be much more careful than we are, not only as to what we do and say, but also what we think. Will you try to be more so in future? Will you, whenever you are tempted to do anything wrong, try to remember that although no one may be near you, no human eye may see you, God is looking down upon you; and that your sin, whatever it may be, though it may be concealed from your fellow-creatures, cannot be hidden from Him, but will be taken account of and brought against you at the great Day of Judgment.

There is no escaping from the presence of the Lord for us any more than there was for Jonah; for "His eyes are upon the ways of man, and He seeth all his goings[b]." We may indeed sin unknown to any human being, but not unknown to God. Many are tempted to do under cover of darkness what they would not dare to do in broad daylight with other people looking on. Ah! they forget that the darkness is no darkness with Him; it is as clear as the day: the darkness and light to Him are both alike. Do not you do so.

Try to recollect that He is always present with you. Say to yourself, "Doth not He see my ways, and count all my steps[c]?" and

[b] Job xxxiv. 21. [c] Job xxxi. 4.

let this thought make you more watchful over yourself, more careful to live, as ever in His sight.

> " All day long an Eye is o'er us,
> Which our every secret knows;
> Sees our every step before us,
> From first morn till evening's close;"

—even the eye of the All-seeing God. Think of this often, and pray to Him to purify and sanctify your hearts by His Holy Spirit, and to give you such an abiding sense of His presence with you, that you may not dare to sin against Him by thought, word, or deed.

> " O Lord, whate'er our guilt may be,
> We cannot from Thy presence flee.
> Help us to feel that Thou art nigh,
> Though hid from every human eye:
>
> At work or play, by day or night,
> That we are ever in Thy sight.
> Let this thought dwell our hearts within,
> And keep us from the ways of sin."

XXII.

The Birds of the Air.

DO you know anything about birds? Of course you do. Such of you as live in the country could tell me the names of numbers of them; and not only their names, but how and where they build their nests, what they live upon, and all about their ways and habits. And those who live in towns can tell me something, if not so much, about them; for wherever there are trees, or a garden, if it be ever such a little bit, there will be birds of some kind—sparrows at any rate, if there are no others. You may see dozens of them, any day, skimming about in the air, and hear them singing with all their might in the trees and hedges in summer time; and in the winter, I daresay you have often watched them hopping about near the houses, picking up stray crumbs, and anything else they can find in the way of food, and twittering and chirping as gaily as ever.

Have you not sometimes wondered how they manage to live all through the cold weather, when the fruits and berries are gone, and the trees and bushes are leafless and bare, and thought they must be starved when the frost and snow came? If you have not, it must have been because you remembered the words of the Lord Jesus, "Behold the fowls of the air: they sow not, neither do they reap, nor gather into barns; yet your Heavenly Father feedeth them[a]." Yes; it is God who takes care of them, and gives them food and shelter: the great and good God, who cares for and watches over every creature He has made,—whose "mercy is over all His works[b]."

Poor little helpless, worthless things they seem to us, and we do not think it of any consequence whether they live or die; and

[a] Matt. vi. 26. [b] Psalm cxlv. 9.

yet our Lord tells us that "not one of them is forgotten before God[c]."

And why does He tell us this? To teach us something about His goodness and mercy towards ourselves. To teach us that the same loving Father who takes thought for them, watches over us, and provides for all our wants. He, who is the giver of every good gift, sends us all we need,—food, clothing, and shelter, health, strength, friends, and overy other blessing we possess. He keeps us from harm, and makes us to dwell in safety. He it is who preserves us from "the pestilence that walketh in darkness, and from the sickness that destroyeth in the noon-day[d]." Surely we ought to be very grateful to Him for all these mercies; but do you think we really are so? I am afraid not. I fear we are all too apt to take our daily comforts as a matter of course, and very seldom think of the God who bestows them on us, or thank Him for doing so. We seem to think

[c] Luke xii. 6.

[d] Psalm xci. 6.

it quite natural that we should be always well and strong, and rarely value health and strength as His gifts, until He teaches us to do so by sending us pain and sickness; and as long as no harm happens to us, no sudden accident befals us, we too often forget that we owe our safety to Him.

This, then, is one lesson which our Lord means us to learn from the birds of the air, —a lesson of thankfulness; but there is yet another,—a lesson of trust. They cannot lay up any store of provisions for themselves, they depend upon what God pleases to send them day by day; and so our Saviour tells us that we must not be too anxious about the things of this world, and think more of providing for our bodily wants and comforts than anything else, but must take thankfully what God pleases to send us, and trust to Him for all else that we need.

"Consider the ravens: for they neither sow nor reap; which neither have storehouse nor barn; and God feedeth them: how much more are ye better than the fowls[e]?" As He "feedeth the young ravens that call upon Him[f]," so will He send you all things that are needful both for your souls and bodies.

> "God hears the hungry lions howl,
> He feeds the raven hoarse and grey;
> Cares He alone for beast and fowl?
> Are we less dear than they?"

Do not think that this cannot apply to you because you have a home to shelter you and parents to provide for you: it will not always be so. Your parents may die and leave no provision for you: or if they are spared to you, sooner or later the time will come when you must go out into the world and get your own living in some way or other. And if it please God to bless your endeavours and make you prosperous, let the birds of the air teach you not to think too much about, or care too much for, the necessaries and comforts of this life, lest you forget

[e] Luke xii. 24. [f] Psalm cxlvii. 9.

or grow careless about the things which concern your soul. But if your lot be cast among the poor and needy, learn from these same birds to cast all your care upon Him. They wait upon Him and He giveth them "their meat in due season[g]:" just so will He give you each day your daily bread, if you ask Him for it in humble faith.

Above all, remember who it is that gives you all the blessings you now enjoy. Never go to rest without thanking Him for all the mercies of the past day, and asking His protection while you sleep; and when you rise in the morning, thank Him for having preserved you through the night, and brought you in health and safety to the beginning of another day, and ask Him to keep you from all hurtful things, and give you all those things which are profitable for you. Beg Him to fill you with such gratitude for all His mercies, that you may ever love and serve Him with all your heart, with all your

[g] Psalm civ. 27.

mind, and with all your strength; and shew forth His praise, not only with your lips, but in your lives; by giving up yourselves to His service, and by walking before Him in holiness and righteousness all your days, through Jesus Christ our Lord.

"Nay, Christian child, kneel down and own
The Hand that feeds Thee day by day,
Nor, careless, with thy lip alone
For 'all things needful' pray.

"The lion and the raven die—
They only ask life's common bread;
Our souls shall live eternally,
And they too must be fed.

"Then not alone for earthly food
Teach us with lisping tongue to pray;—
The heavenly meat that makes us good,
Lord, give us day by day."

XXIII.

The Flowers of the Field.

I AM sure you all of you love flowers; I never knew a child who did not. I have never known any child who did not delight to ramble in the woods and lanes, and come home laden with wild flowers. I never see a child pass even the commonest flowers growing by the road-side, without stopping to gather a handful of them. I daresay you have all of you, many a time, spent hours in the fields, weaving daisies into chains and necklaces, making cowslip balls, searching the hedges for violets, or making posies of all the flowers you could find.

And how lovely they are! Who does not rejoice when the primroses peep out, like pale yellow stars, telling us that the winter is over and gone, and the spring is come?

And the modest violet, hiding its head beneath the clustering leaves, and filling the air with its delicious perfume; the graceful fern, the stately fox-glove, and the delicate harebell; the buttercups, yellow as gold, and the daisies, nestling, like silver stars, in the grass at our feet. All these, and many more as fair and sweet, you must have gathered many and many a time; but when doing so did you ever stop to think who made them? who shaped their delicate leaves, painted their lovely blossoms with such brilliant colours, and placed each plant just where it will grow best, and have sunshine or shade as is best for it?

There are many flowers more gorgeous, but not more beautiful,—flowers which are only within the reach of rich people; for although God made them too, they are costly to buy, and more so to keep; for they require to be sheltered from the cold, and shaded from the heat, and must be watched, and trained, and tended constantly, to bring them to perfection. But these wild flowers grow everywhere, and within the reach of all; making the whole earth bright and beautiful even where no human eye can see them.

It is true that God has given them to delight our eyes and gladden our hearts, but do you think this is all? Oh no! He means them, as He does everything else He has made, to teach us something about Him, and something about ourselves. And about Him, they teach us, first, His power. Which of us, the wisest and cleverest among us, could make anything so perfect and beautiful as the simplest flower that grows by the wayside? Not one. We might, perhaps, imitate it as far as the outward form is concerned, but it would be *only* an imitation: we could not impart fragrance to it; we could not give it life, and make it bloom again and again, year after year, as He does.

More than this, they shew His love and

care in providing for the wants of all His creatures; for insects feed upon the leaves of plants, and you know the honey which the bees make from the flowers in the summer serves them for food during the winter: besides which, some of them serve as fodder for cattle; and many birds and animals feed upon their roots and seeds.

Then they teach us something about ourselves. And first they teach us a lesson of trust, as our Blessed Saviour Himself tells us. Hear what He says about it: "Consider the lilies of the field, how they grow; they toil not, neither do they spin: and yet I say unto you, That Solomon in all his glory was not arrayed like one of these. Wherefore, if God so clothe the grass of the field, which to-day is, and to-morrow is cast into the oven, shall He not much more clothe you, O ye of little faith? Therefore take no thought, saying, What shall we eat? or, What shall we drink? or, Wherewithal shall we be clothed? . . . . But seek ye first the kingdom of God, and

His righteousness; and all these things shall be added unto you[a]."

And by this our Lord means to teach us, that just as God clothes the flowers with beauty, and sends them sunshine and dew to nourish and refresh them, so He will send us "all things needful both for our souls and bodies," if we trust to Him for them; "for your Heavenly Father knoweth that ye have need of all these things." He does not mean that we are to take no thought at all for food or raiment, but that we must not think too much of them, and so let the "cares of this world and the deceitfulness of riches" fill our heart and drive the love of Him out of it.

Then they teach us another lesson—a lesson of content. They do not envy the flowers that grow in gardens and hot-houses, if they are ever so much grander, and larger, and gayer than they are; but go on blooming in the fields and hedges, the woods and thickets,—often on mountains or in deserts, where no

[a] Matt. vi. 28—33.

eye but His own ever sees them,—through the heat of summer and the cold of winter, fulfilling His will.

"Day by day the little daisy
  Looks up with its yellow eye,
Never murmurs, never wishes
  It were hanging up on high.

"God has given each his station;
  Some have riches and high place,
Some have lowly homes and labour,—
  All may have His precious grace."

So if ever you feel tempted to be discontented with your lot, and to think that you would be better off in any other station or place, try to remember that God has placed you just where you are, because He knows it to be the best place for you. Try to learn the lessons He would teach you by the flowers of the field; and pray for "His precious grace" to profit by them, and put them into practice. Pray that He will help you, by His Holy Spirit, to serve Him faithfully and contentedly in your place, as they do in theirs.

"They have no proud, no foolish thoughts,
Because they are so fair;
They wish for nothing, quite content
With sunshine and sweet air.

"God gave to them their colours bright,
To us, faith, hope, and love,
And bade us fear the things of earth,
And seek the things above."

XXIV.

Idle Words.

IDLE words! How soon they are uttered; and how apt we are to think them of no consequence! And yet if we turn to the Bible we find that our Blessed Lord did not think so; for He tells us that "Every idle word that men shall speak, they shall give account thereof in the day of judgment[a]."

Is not that an awful thought, when we remember how often we all offend in this respect? Just think for one moment; try to recollect all you have said this day; and I am sure your own conscience will remind you of many an idle word, beside many which you may have forgotten, but which are not forgotten before God. Perhaps you think that there can be no harm in any words that fall

[a] Matt. xii. 36.

short of lying, swearing, and blaspheming; but that is a great mistake. You may neither lie, nor swear, nor blaspheme yourself, but some careless word of yours may lead some one else to commit any or all of these sins; and then, although you may never know in this life that it did so, that idle word will rise up and witness against you at the last great Day.

We often hear and read of a few hasty words leading to bloodshed. I will tell you of one instance in which they did so.

There was once a King of England who never could agree with the clergy; and he was, more especially, always quarrelling with the Archbishop of Canterbury, who held the highest rank in the Church. One day, the King happened to hear of something the Archbishop had done which made him very angry indeed; and in his passion, he said he wished some one would rid him of this man. Four of his followers who had heard this, armed themselves, and set off directly in search of the Archbishop; and when they found him, which they did in his own cathedral, fell upon him and killed him at the foot of the altar. Now the King did not really mean what he said in his anger, and repented bitterly when he found his hasty words had led his followers to commit such a cruel murder: but that was of no use. His repentance would not bring the poor Archbishop back to life, and so the sin belonged quite as much to him as to those who actually committed it. Truly, as Solomon says, "Death and life are in the power of the tongue[b]." There is never any knowing what mischief may be worked by a few thoughtless words; and once said, they cannot be recalled, if you repent them ever so bitterly. So you must guard against all sorts of idle words; tale-bearing; uncharitable words; bitter, scornful words; foolish gossip and chatter about other people and their affairs; lightness and levity of speech: for although you may not mean any harm, and

[b] Prov. xviii. 21.

may be talking merely for talking's sake, you may not be able to stop there, and so may be led into sin.

St. James tells us that "the tongue is a fire, a world of iniquity:" that "it setteth on fire the whole course of nature," and is itself "set on fire of hell." That "every kind of beasts, and of birds, and of serpents, and of things in the sea, is tamed, and hath been tamed of mankind; but the tongue can no man tame: it is an unruly evil, full of deadly poison[c]." And surely when, instead of being used for the praise and glory of God, it is used for cursing, and swearing, and railing, we must feel the truth of what the Apostle says concerning it.

Then, again, there is another way in which idle words will condemn us: I mean when we pray to God with our lips, without thinking what we are about, and without really drawing nigh to Him with our hearts. It is very easy to kneel down and say a few

[c] James iii. 6—8.

words of prayer, without thinking at all about God or feeling that we are in His presence: and then, though we may think that we are praying, we are only uttering vain words to our own condemnation, and sinning against Him by taking His Name in vain.

Watch, then, over your heart, for "out of the abundance of the heart the mouth speaketh[d]." Watch very carefully over your tongue, and try to remember that God hears every word you say. Pray, as David did, that He will "set a watch before your mouth, and keep the door of your lips," that you may not sin against Him with your tongue: and that the words of your lips and the meditation of your heart may be always acceptable in His sight.

"Watch our lips and guard them, Lord;
Check the rash and idle word;
Turn our feet, whene'er we stray,
Lead us in the perfect way."

[d] Luke vi. 45.

XXV.

Rich and Poor.

IF you were asked whether you would rather be rich or poor, I fancy you would most of you, if not all, say "rich," if you spoke the honest truth. I daresay you think it must be very delightful to have handsome houses and carriages, servants to wait upon you, fine clothes, plenty to eat and drink, and plenty of money to do as you like with. And perhaps when you have seen any one with all these things, you have been tempted to envy them, and feel discontented that you had none of them; at any rate, you have doubtless thought they were much better off than you; — maybe they have thought so themselves.

And if this world were to last for ever, if there were no Heaven or Hell to come afterwards, it might be so; though even then riches could not keep from you sorrow, pain, sickness, and death. But we know that we must all die one day; and when that day comes, who will be the best off? Not those who have been rich, and had everything they could desire in this life; but those who have been content with what God has seen fit to give them, be it ever so little, and have striven to serve and please Him instead of pleasing themselves.

You may think that you could do this all the same for being rich; that you might even be able to do it better: but just listen to what our Lord Jesus Christ says about this. "How hardly shall they that have riches enter into the kingdom of God[a]!"—those are His very words. And why does He say so? Because He knows how easily we are turned away from Him. He knows that, with riches, the love of money and of the pomps and vanities of the world will creep into our heart,

[a] Mark x. 23.

and leave no room in it for the love of God: and so, although He does not say that the rich *cannot* enter into the kingdom of heaven, He says they can only do it "hardly,"—that is, with difficulty.

You must not, however, think that all rich people are wicked, or that all poor people are good: it is not so in either case. The mere *having* riches is only dangerous, and often hurtful to the soul: it is the coveting them, the trying to get them by any means, the caring for them above everything else, that is sinful. There are some, indeed, to whom God has given wealth, who look upon it as a talent He has committed to their charge, and try to make use of it in His service and for His glory. But we, most of us, like living in ease and luxury better than faring hardly and denying ourselves; and when we have everything we can wish for in this world, we are apt to forget all about any other,—aye, even to forget God Himself,—and to think of nothing but our own comfort and pleasure; and this is just what our Blessed Lord tells us we must *not* do. He says, "Ye cannot serve God and mammon[b]." He tells us that if we would follow Him, we must deny ourselves, and take up our cross; and as riches hinder, or prevent our doing this, surely it is better to be without them. "What shall it profit a man, if he shall gain the whole world, and lose his own soul[c]?" Well may we pray, as we do in the words of the Litany, not "in all time of our tribulation" only, but "in all time of our wealth, Good Lord, deliver us."

You know St. Paul tells us, "They that will be rich fall into temptation and a snare, and into many foolish and hurtful lusts, which drown men in destruction and perdition[d]." They that *will* be rich—that is, those who long to be rich; whose chief, if not only care, is how to become so. Bear this warning in mind, "Seek first" the true riches which last for ever, even "the kingdom of God and

[b] Matt. vi. 24. [c] Mark viii. 36.

[d] 1 Tim. vi. 9.

His righteousness," and leave the rest to Him. He knows what is best for every one of us; and whatever our lot in life may be, we may be sure it is just that which is best for us, whether rich or poor.

> "God made thy cottage home so dear,
> Gave store enough for frugal fare;
> If richer homes have better cheer,
> 'Twas God who sent it there."

Hunger and thirst, cold and weariness are hard to bear, but if these are your portion, remember that our Blessed Lord bore them all for your sake. "Ye know the grace of our Lord Jesus Christ, that, though He was rich, yet for your sakes He became poor, that ye through His poverty might be rich[a]."

> "He had no glory here on earth,
> No riches, and no state;
> His Christian children must not care
> For being rich or great.

> "Fine clothes, fine houses, pretty things,
> That please our longing eyes,
> Would only make our hearts forget
> Our treasure in the skies."

[a] 2 Cor. viii. 9.

If you are friendless, remember that He is your Friend, and loves you better than any earthly friend could do. If you are homeless, think that when on earth He had not "where to lay His head[f]." Think of that glorious home in heaven which He has prepared for all His children; all who truly love and serve Him, whether rich or poor. You may be poor enough in this world's good, but that matters little if you are rich towards God. "Lay not up for yourselves treasures upon earth, where moth and rust doth corrupt, and where thieves break through and steal: but lay up for yourselves treasures in heaven, where neither moth nor rust doth corrupt, and where thieves do not break through nor steal: for where your treasure is, there will your heart be also[g]." Pray that He will keep you from the sin of covetousness: that He will grant you the riches of His grace, and help you to serve Him faithfully, and do your duty with a contented mind in that

[f] Matt. viii. 20. [g] Matt. vi. 19—21.

station of life to which He has been pleased to call you.

"You must be content and quiet,
Your appointed stations in;
For to envy, or to covet
Others' goods, is mortal sin.

"And God loveth all His children,
Rich and poor, and high and low;
And they all shall meet in heaven,
Who have served Him here below."

XXVI.

Harvest.

WHAT a pleasant sight to look upon is a harvest-field! The yellow corn waving in the breeze like a sea of gold; the groups of reapers scattered about, hard at work with the sickle, binding up the sheaves, or taking their noon-day meal under shelter of the hedge; and the bright sunshine over all. I daresay you have often seen such a sight; maybe have done many a good day's gleaning, have followed in the train of the wagon which carried home the last sheaf, and joined afterwards in the Harvest-home, or Thanksgiving Feast, which follows when the work is done; have shared in "the joy of harvest." Surely it should make us both joyful and thankful when God is pleased to bless the fruits of the earth and send us plenty of food.

HARVEST.

Is it not wonderful to think of the little seed buried in the earth, and the young plant springing from it in silence and darkness, and making its way unseen, but slowly and surely, up to the surface of the ground, growing taller and stronger day by day: first the blade, then the ear, after that the full corn in the ear, until it is ripe enough to be cut down and stored away, to be made into food for man? Is it not still more wonderful to think that this has been going on ever since the world and the earth were made? Year by year has the seed been sown, and the crop raised and reaped; and year after year will it be the same, we know, as long as the world shall last: for God Himself has given us the promise that "While the earth remaineth, seedtime and harvest, and cold and heat, and summer and winter, and day and night shall not cease[a]." Try to think of this whenever you take a walk through the fields, and let it make you more mindful of His

[a] Gen. viii. 22.

mercy and goodness. But there is something more that I want you to call to mind too. You know that if we will but try to learn it, there is some lesson to be learnt from all God's works. He means to teach us something about heavenly things by means of earthly things, even the common things which we see, and which take place around us every day of our lives. All the parables of our Lord shew us this clearly enough; and in one of them (I daresay you know which it is) He tells His disciples that "the field is the world; the harvest is the end of the world; and the reapers are the angels[b]." I should think they never passed a cornfield afterwards without thinking of these words: and that is what He meant they should do, what He means us to do too.

Everybody knows that in the field where only wheat is sown, weeds and other hurtful things, such as tares, come up; and concerning this He tells us that "the good seed are

[b] Matt. xiii. 38, 39.

the children of the kingdom"—His children; but "the tares are the children of the wicked one." Dear children, among which will you be found in that day? Will you be gathered in with the wheat by the heavenly reapers, or cast in among the tares by the Lord of the harvest? Who can say? All we know is, that as the wheat and the tares are suffered to go on growing together until the harvest, so will it be with us until the last great day, when "the angels shall come forth and sever the wicked from among the just[c]." We can only strive to love and serve Him now, and pray for acceptance then for Christ's sake.

Think how awful it would be to be cast out from His presence for evermore! And if we are it will be our own fault. He willeth not that any should perish. He "so loved the world, that He gave His only-begotten Son, that whosoever believeth in Him should not perish, but have everlasting life[d]." And

[c] Matt. xiii. 49. [d] John iii. 16.

Jesus loves us, and is ever ready to help us if we will but turn to him. But if we will *not* do this,—if we *will* go on sinning against Him instead of loving and serving Him willingly, and trying to please Him here,—if we will not have Him for our Master in this world, He will not have us for His children in heaven.

Think of this often, and pray constantly and fervently that He will give you grace so perfectly to love and faithfully to serve Him now, that you may not fear to meet Him then; but may be numbered among those who are accepted for His sake, and gathered into His kingdom in heaven to dwell with Him for ever.

"What is earth but God's own field,
Fruit unto His praise to yield?
Wheat and tares therein are sown,
Unto joy or sorrow grown;
Ripening with a wondrous power,
Till the final harvest-hour:
Grant, O Lord of life, that we
Holy grain and pure may be."

CPSIA information can be obtained
at www.ICGtesting.com
Printed in the USA
LVHW022004120422
716028LV00006B/358

9 783752 594843